WEIRD MAGAZINE

Weird House Press © 2022

Weird House Press
Joe Morey, Publisher
Central Point, OR USA
www.weirdhousepress.com

EDITORS
Curtis M. Lawson
Joe Morey

Weird House Magazine layout, design, cover art, and story header art by Cyrusfiction Productions

Nick Greenwood grants Weird House Press one-time rights to publish all the artwork in issue #1 of Weird House Magazine © 2022.

SHORT STORIES © 2022 by the authors
The City of Frozen Shadows by Tim Curran
Freshest Catch by Carol Gyzander
The Gravedigger's Tale by Simon Clark
Gallows of Hell by Curtis M. Lawson
Melissa and the Stone Troll by Elana Gomel
Eternity by Elana Gomel
Black Grief by Aaron Besson
The House That Wanted To Die by Joshua Rex
The Restless Quill by Scott Thomas

POETRY COPYRIGHT © 2022 by the authors
Ann K. Schwader
David Barker

INTERVIEWS © 2022 by the authors
Interview with Tim Curran
Interview with Nick Greenwood

NONFICTION © 2022 by the authors
Editorial, by Curtis M. Lawson
Musicians on Horror by Curtis M. Lawson
The Lingering Horror of Silent Hill by Robert Ottone
Color out of Space: A Review by Gary Hill
What I Look For In Weird Poetry by F. J. Bergman

EDITORIAL
A Note From the Editor 3

FICTION AND POETRY
The City of Frozen Shadow
  by Tim Curran 4
Poetry by Ann K. Schwader 20
Freshest Catch by Carol Gyzander 26
The Gravedigger's Tale
  by Simon Clark 43
Gallows of Hell
  by Curtis M. Lawson 55
Poetry by David Barker 65
Melissa and the Stone Troll
  by Elana Gomel 70
Eternity by Elana Gomel 72
Black Grief by Aaron Besson 91
The House That Wanted to Die
  by Joshua Rex 100
The Restless Quill by Scott Thomas 106

FEATURES
An interview with Tim Curran 15
What I Look For In Weird Poetry
  by F. J. Bergman 24
The Lingering Terror of Silent Hill
  by Robert Ottone 36
Musicians on Horror
  by Curtis M. Lawson 51
An Interview With Nick Greenwood 76
Weird House Showcase:
  The Artwork of Nick Greenwood. 83
The Color Out of Space: a review
  by Gary Hill 96

ISSUE No. 1
JUNE 2022
https://www.weirdhousepress.com

Weird House
a specialty horror press
Order from weirdhousepress.com

THE SKINLESS FACE
by Donald Tyson

A unique journey into dreamworlds of terror ...

14 spine-tingling excursions into realms of nightmare in the tradition of H. P. Lovecraft, with two full-length novellas never before published.

In "The Skinless Face," archaeologists investigate a lost civilization of the Gobi Desert. Why did this ancient race chisel off the face of their stone god and bury it beneath the sands? "The Waves Beckon" when a nurse takes a job in a sanatorium in the New England town of Innsmouth. She discovers that the ancient curse from the sea hanging over the community has left a horrifying legacy. On a remote little island in John Dee Lake, four friends discover to their horror that "The Thing On the Island" was buried there centuries ago for a reason. What happens when the world goes insane? In "The Organ of Chaos," society falls into unspeakable practices and the worship of alien gods. A young woman taking a position as a Victorian governess looks forward to the voyage across the Atlantic, but discovers that she has booked a "Forbidden Passage."

Prepare for a reading experience unlike any other. These fears and more await you in this exquisitely selected horror collection from the fertile and terrifying imagination of Donald Tyson.

Trade paperback and ebook editions at Amazon.com

The Dreaming Man by William Meikle
Holmes Is Back!

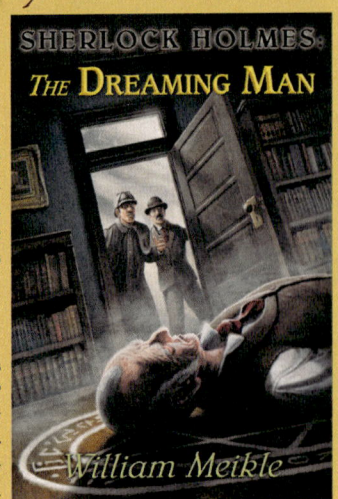

A mystery that starts in the House of Lords leads Holmes and Watson the length of England, uncovering a plot that might bring down the British Empire. To solve the case, Holmes must come to grips with a revenant spirit, who bends his iron will to returning from the dead. A fall is coming that has haunted Holmes' dreams and now must be faced again, in the place where past and present become one, and two old foes meet for a final battle.

Praise for Willam Miekle

"For anyone who loves great storytelling and well-crafted stories." —Famous Monsters of Filmland

"Meikle writes Holmes and Watson with a warm friendship." —Horrorview

"The plots are well conceived and the narrative style elegant and effective. Baker Street Irregulars should quickly secure a copy." —British Fantasy Society

"... a splendid and entertaining diversion." —Black Static

Purchase the beautifully designed hardcover at weirdhousepress.com

For a 10% Discount code on your next weirdhousepress.com order use code: THANKYOU

Trade paperback and ebook editions at Amazon.com

A Note From the Editor

Welcome to the first issue of Weird House Magazine! We appreciate you spending your leisure time with us and allowing us to showcase some of the most gifted talents in dark fiction. We know there are a million books, movies, and video games out there, and we appreciate you joining us in this old-fashioned format.

What should you expect? Well, let's be clear that we wouldn't call ourselves a literary journal or anything quite so serious. There are lots of great publishers putting out thoughtful criticism, analysis, and deep insights about horror and weird fiction. They do a great job, so we decided to go a different route. What you hold in your hand is primarily a pulp magazine, with a dash of *Rolling Stone* thrown in. The fiction comes first, but we'll also be doing interviews, talking with artists from adjacent mediums, and featuring articles about film, games, and more.

I suppose if I had to pick one word for the tone of Weird House Magazine, it would be *escape*. Sit back and enjoy a good yarn (or five), hang out with your favorite authors, and take your mind off the world for a little bit. And who knows, maybe you'll discover your new favorite story along the way.

Part of what we want to do is help present authors and literary folks as the rock stars that we see them as. I think a good place to start is our editor/publisher/founder, Joe Morey (if he lets me print this).

Joe Morey has been publishing small press books for nearly 40 years. He has helped launch the careers of countless authors (myself included) and has worked with many of the most important names in horror/weird fiction. As the founder of Dark Regions Press, which he ran from 1985 - 2013, then Dark Renaissance, and finally Weird House, Joe has published the work of Ramsey Campbell, Simon Clark, Tony Richard, Donald Tyson, W. H. Pugmire, and many other giants in the field.

In the early days of Dark Regions, Joe an experienced pressman, would not only publish books but also roll up his sleeves and physically print them. Around that same time, he put together Dark Regions magazine, which featured the work of luminaries such as Brian Lumley, Michael Bishop, and Bruce Boston. From the humble roots of churning out zines and books on his own printing press, he went on to win the HWA Specialty Press Award and to make a name publishing truly beautiful and unique hardcover editions of fabulous stories.

It is not hyperbole to say that Joe Morey's impact on horror literature is just as substantial as that of high-profile dark fiction editors like S. T. Joshi, Stephen Jones, and Ellen Datlow. He has and continues to be a force for growth, excellence, and kindness in our community. It is a true honor to work alongside Joe on this project, as well as others.

With all that said, I hope that you, dear reader, enjoy the first issue of Weird House Magazine as much as we enjoyed creating it. Thanks for reading and stay weird!

—*Curtis M. Lawson*
Providence, RI 2022

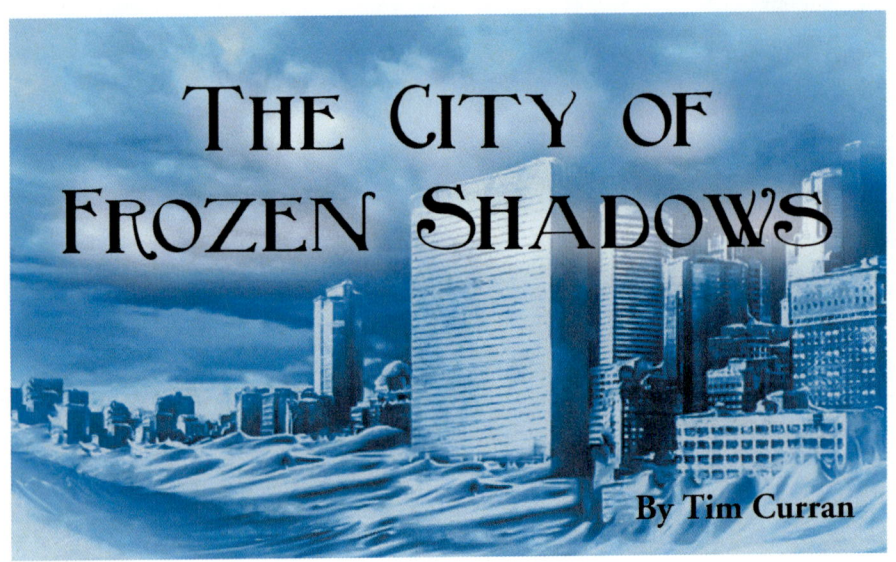

The City of Frozen Shadows

By Tim Curran

The city was silent.

Blown by frigid winds, its streets and thoroughfares were barren as night came on. Trees were denuded and gnarled. No grass grew. No cats prowled. No night birds flew. Machinery was abandoned and houses were weathered gray, silent as bones. The stars looked down cold and pitiless and only ghosts walked its streets.

It was a graveyard.

§

Alone.

Charles Taylor was alone.

Alone in the dead urban moonscape. A pitted and gouged netherworld of shadowy buildings that were hulking, crumbling monoliths from a decayed and deceased civilization. Those that had built them were mummies now, drained of warmth and life and discarded like empty cans. All of them had been put to bed, tucked into sarcophagi and kissed by dust.

Taylor had red blood in his veins. He was alive and he was the last of the free men. Or at least this was what he told himself. It was easier that way.

The darkness was heavy and waiting, the wind cold. It was always cold. The world was wrapped in heavy cloud cover now. Light could penetrate it, but not heat. Nuclear winter. It had been this way for a year now since the Stygans came, since they had made Earth like their own world—frozen and stark.

He pressed himself into the shadows of the buildings, a 9mm

automatic in his fist, a .38 in his coat pocket. He carried a knife, too. He was not afraid to use them. It had been quiet for days now and he did not like that. The hunters were out there somewhere. They looked like men and women and children, but they were not human. Mannequins animated by their alien puppet masters. Nothing more.

He thought: *The last one? Am I really the last one? The last breath of life in this sterile world?*

He looked up and down the streets. The city was effused with a surreal glow from the brooding, ancient moon above. He dashed from his hiding place and sought the shadows near a row of abandoned cars. He crept along them like a cat. In the distance he heard the peculiar sharp whirring of the alien war machines. They patrolled the streets and the fact that they still did said something. If he were the last man, why would the death machines keep up the vigil?

He licked his lips and his breath frosted into the night.

Sometimes he thought it was all a game with them. They had superior technology. No doubt they had methods of scanning, technologies probably light-years beyond infra-red. So why didn't they just pick up his heat signature and do away with him? He should have been easy to spot in the ice sculpture of the city.

He lit a cigarette, daring them to find him. His disobedience was a raw and hurting sore to them. Or, at least, he hoped so.

It was at times like this when the loneliness lay on him like concrete that he found himself thinking about Barbara. They were married two months when the shit rained down from the stars. And in love, oh God, how they'd been in—

Enough.

He couldn't think like that. Barbara was dead. She was part of the past.

Taylor grimaced with hate. The hatred cleared his head.

His face had long ago gone to leather from the bitter temperatures. His beard was thick and full. With the black watch cap pulled down over his ears, he looked like a burglar. But that was fine because he was one. It was how he made his living before they came and even now, crouched alongside a minivan, his pack was filled with cans of food he'd stolen.

Stolen?

No, it was hardly—

Quiet.

Yes, they were coming. A group of hunters. He sucked in a breath. His teeth wanted to chatter and his belly was filled with crawling things. He heard their footsteps. They did not speak. They marched with military efficiency, searching out stragglers. He saw them spill onto the avenue, five shapes cut from black cloth. Machines. Drones. They moved as one, remorseless, merciless, unrelenting.

They walked past the row of vehicles and stopped.

Taylor did not breath.

His heart did not beat.

His cells did not divide.

He went to stone and waited. Oh, God, he'd gotten so good at waiting, at silence. Only a marble bust was better at it. The hunters stood there, still as graveyard statues, all staring up the street. Then… they suddenly turned their heads in his direction, but all at the same time like they were hooked into a central brain. Which, they were. Dead, yes, they were all dead as such. Chips in their brains now. Their physiologies forever altered by alien biomedical technology.

Taylor knew he had to make a break for it.

He slowly backed into the oily pool of shadows cast by a Savings and Loan building. And they saw him right away. He knew by long experience that they did not hunt by sight or sound or even body heat, but by motion. And even the motion of lungs or the action of a heart muscle was enough. They could not pinpoint you, but they knew you were near.

One of them, a woman, spotted him.

Her eyes were huge and glistening red like pools of blood. No pupils, just black-red orbs swimming in unblinking sockets. She jabbed a finger at him and made a dry, hissing sound. The others began to hiss now, too. Like human insects, like locusts.

Taylor stood his ground, drawing them in like a fly into a web.

They fanned out, hissing like tea kettles, staring and pointing and hungry for the warmth that was in him. He let them get in closer. Their faces were pallid and etched by frost, painted yellow by the glacial moon. He kept the 9mm against his leg, made no threatening moves. They came on like marauding ants anxious to strip the carcass of an injured mouse.

Closer.

He smiled. "Not this time, assholes," he said under his breath.

When they were maybe ten feet away and he was certain he could not miss, he opened up. The automatic jerked in his gloved fist, gouts of flame spitting from the barrel. A man took two slugs that spun him around into another. A woman took hers in the belly. Her partner caught one in the chest, another in the throat. Taylor kept firing until they were all down and pissing that cold green sap they called blood.

They were all silent then, except one woman.

Half of her face hung from a grizzled thread of blasted flesh. Her lips pulled away from even, white teeth, eyes glowing with a malefic, cheated hatred. She began to hiss as gouts of green fluid spilled from her mouth. Her wounds steamed in the air.

Taylor shot her between the eyes.

The night grew heavy and black.

He wasn't worried about the hunters he'd drilled.

He'd greased them in a neighborhood far from his own. He'd only been there scavenging. Let them bring in their machines, let them level it. He was far away, laughing because maybe he was simply tired of crying. And killing them was the only true pleasure he had left. And this month, he'd clipped seventeen so far.

Fuck 'em.

He kept telling himself there had to be others. Brothers and sisters with warmth in their veins and fight in their hearts, comrades in the resistance. If he had survived, so had others.

§

His life was a tight, ceaseless circle of grim repetition.

Only through habit, through disciplined routine, had he survived this long. Nothing was left to chance. Impulse was unthinkable. All had to be plotted out—when to leave his hideout, when to gather food, when to sleep, when to eat, when to search for others.

Shortly after he'd gone into hiding, he'd raided a National Guard armory. He had handguns, grenades, automatic rifles, submachine guns, even perimeter mines. Things he'd used when he was a soldier years before. For a time, he'd booby-trapped old houses and buildings, leaving little surprises for the hunters. He only stopped when he thought he might accidentally kill living men or women.

§

He was sitting in the bombed-out ruin of a tenement. Waiting, smoking, watching the streets below through a missing section of wall. Watching the moon lord over the city. In the distance, he could hear the war machines. But not too often. Not like a few months ago.

Time to move.

He made sure his guns were loaded and ready, that his knife slid easily from its oiled sheath. *Check.* He stood up. There was a figure leaning up against a pile of rubble. Just sitting there, maybe trying to blend in.

A hunter?

He didn't think so, but he had to be sure. He slid his knife from its sheath. It was a K-bar. A fighting knife favored by the U.S. Marines once upon a time. It had a black, rubberized handle and a blue-steel blade, seven-inches long and sharp enough to slit a hair lengthwise.

He moved quickly and quietly like a cat.

The figure sat in a somewhat precarious position, back against the rubble, feet dangling into the night where the wall had once been. And nothing below but a three-story drop.

Taylor was careful.

He knew the Stygans liked to set out traps, baiting them with flesh and blood humans. More than once he'd been sucked into such a scenario. Once, they had used a child. Unthinkable, but it was how they were—cold, alien intellects that treated humans like insects to be used or crushed.

He came up on his quarry after he was certain there were no hunters hiding in the shadows. The figure was a man. He saw that much. He came up quick and put his knife against his throat. But he was too late—the guy was already dead. Maybe tonight, maybe last night, he'd slit his wrists.

"Why couldn't you have waited for me?" Taylor said to him. "One more night? A few hours? Would it have been that long?"

But he knew the lonely desperation of solitude, of being the sole survivor. He envied him. Envied his peace, his escape, his strength. He forced his hands away from the man's throat. The body tipped and fell into the night before he could stop it. It hit the walk below and shattered like glass.

And that, he knew, was more than mere cold. You didn't freeze-up like that from the wind. The Stygans had been at him. They had touched him. Whenever they touched someone, they went to ice, to crystal like they'd been dipped in liquid oxygen.

He remembered finding Barbara like that and how she'd broken apart as he touched her.

Taylor slumped over and wept.

The world was dead.

And death had come from the stars. But it hadn't come with flying saucers or comic book destruction, it had come quietly.

§

The old SETI network had picked up the first signal.

They called it a hyper-light transmission. It nearly overloaded their computers and took weeks to sort out the mathematical language. Finally, all the money spent searching the heavens for neighbors had paid off. The communication was from a planet called Styga. It was the seventh planet circling a star designated TXK221-B by the aliens, but known to Earth astronomers as Theta Eridani, a binary star, in the constellation of Eridanus, some 160 light- years from earth. They were uncertain as to our location. They wished to know more of our world and its people. They gave the SETI astronomers a precise bandwidth and were told they would amplify our signal in order to speed up the time lag which otherwise could have taken hundreds of years.

The astronomers transmitted the required info.

And the Stygans were never heard from again.

The astronomers promised it would take time, but years and years passed with no further contact. It was puzzling. Disturbing to some militarists who were against the SETI program from the beginning, considering it foolish to be broadcasting our position to anyone who might be listening. An invitation to invasion. And the idea was not simply paranoid, but backed by science. If evolution occurred on alien worlds the way it had on Earth, there could be great danger. For natural selection had generally channeled intellect to predators. Hunting and stalking required tactics, patterns, basic problem-solving—the progenitors of true intelligence.

Five years passed since the original Stygan communication.

It became the butt of jokes, the focus of both paranoia and conspiracy. Then an unthinkable chain of dire events began. A virus invaded Earth's computer systems and nearly overnight, anything with a memory chip in it shut down. Machinery would no longer function. The climate began to grow colder by the day. And lastly, an infectious plague swept the planet. Within a month, what remained of the human race (barely a third of what it had been six weeks before) we're swept into the Stone Age like hairballs into a dustbin. Civilization teetered, than collapsed entirely.

The Stygans arrived a year later in force.

The world was already beaten by then and this with no fancy light shows or Hollywood pyrotechnics. It was only a matter of rounding up the stragglers.

The predators, as it were, had arrived.

§

The hunters were on his trail.

Taylor was running and running, vaulting snowdrifts and skirting patches of black ice. The city reared up cold and dark and silent around him. He saw the subway entrance ahead opening for him like the maw of some primal beast. He slipped down there, waited on the steps with his heart thick in his throat. His lungs were full of fire. He had the 9mm out and he wished to God he'd brought a submachine gun with him.

He listened.

They were coming.

About twenty or thirty of them flowed into the icy streets, bleeding from the shadows. They carried no weapons; they didn't need to. They had formed up in ranks, marching in two single-file columns like automatons. The moonlight was reflected in the mirrored pools of their eyes.

Taylor went down the steps, urging his footfalls to be silent as drifting feathers. Down, down, down. He paused in the freezing darkness. It pooled around him black as tar. He had a flashlight with him, but he didn't dare turn it on. He stood on the platform and the darkness was a palpable thing, grainy, living, breathing. He moved quietly through it. He followed the tiled wall until he found the drop to the tracks. He hopped down there and stalked through the tunnel.

He guided himself using the wall, superstitious terror seizing him. He was alone in the dark…with whatever waited in it. But that was crazy, because there was nothing in the dark. Not anymore. Nothing haunted the dark but ghosts and memories and they were lonely, pale things. He kept pausing and listening, hearing nothing but his labored breathing, the blood rushing in his ears. Maybe, just maybe, he'd gotten lucky. Perhaps they hadn't followed him. He didn't use the subways much because they disturbed him…cave-like, claustrophobic, sunless, like being shut up in a closet or a coffin.

Sucking in a sharp, nervous breath, he dug out his Tekna flashlight and clicked it on. The brilliance of the beam was positively blinding. He saw the tracks winding off into the murk. A smoky haze hung in the air. Motes of dust danced in the beam like drifting moths. He saw a few skeletons heaped in the corner, a jawless skull farther up the track. Things like that had long since ceased to bother him.

Footsteps.

He clicked off the light, a pain ripping through his chest. He could hear their footfalls clearly now, echoing through the underworld. Yes, he'd fooled them for a bit, but now they knew where he'd gone. He heard their footsteps come down the stairs. Light, careful, patient. Then on the platform. He could hear them hissing and whispering. The tunnels caught the sound and amplified it.

He slipped away, boots placed softly, expertly. He moved on, keeping in contact with the stone wall. Sooner or later, he knew, he'd find what he was looking for.

Thud, thud, thud.

They were in the tunnels now, too.

Taylor started moving faster. They could sense motion and they could see in the darkness like hunting cats. He could hear them coming now, stealthily. Their hissings were echoing eerily through the passage. They filled his head with nightmare imagery—anemic faces and huge red eyes, killing fingers and cruel mouths. Close and closer.

He stopped dead.

Up ahead of him, another sound.

A slow, lumbering sound. A dragging noise moving in his direction. More of them? He heard it and then it was gone. His brain, inspired by too many Saturday afternoons of B-Movies, envisioned a giant spider living in the fathomless dark, the tunnels strewn with webs, festooned with dangling human remains.

But there was no time for imagination.

The hunters were very close now. If he squinted his eyes, he could nearly make out their shambling, shadowy forms.

He found a recess in the concrete wall and a door set into it.

He allowed himself to breathe.

A maintenance port.

The door came open, squeaking loudly. He slipped through it, shut it quickly behind him. There was a catch on the inside and he threw it. As he started up the ladder to the world above, he heard them at the door, fists hammering, nails scratching over rusting metal. The hissings and shrilling, and angry whispers. He only wished there was time to booby-trap the ladder.

He moved up it quickly.

It shook and groaned and he was certain it would pull from its cement housing, but it held. He saw light above, a street grating over his head. Shadows latticed his face. He peered through the slats and saw the city, the moon brooding above it full and lonesome. Below, they still worked at the door. They were nothing if not diligent. He swallowed a mouthful of raw fear and pushed at the grating. For a moment or two it wouldn't budge. He kept at it until the ice that welded it in place came free. It clattered onto the sidewalk and he lunged out, rolling through the snow.

Right away he heard the shrill sound of the war machines.

They were coming.

§

One of them prowled from the black mouth of an alley. It looked very much like an elliptical spheroid made of shiny blue-black metal that was crystalline like a diamond. A series of jointed mechanical legs, three on each side, supported it. The first time Taylor saw one he thought Earth had been invaded by giant spiders because that's what they resembled.

He crab-crawled into the shadows.

The war machine knew there was a human nearby, something alive. It moved in his direction, the tips of its legs ringing out with a subtle, hollow clanging as it approached.

Taylor, poised on the edge of a scream, ran into the confines of a crumbling building. A red light from the machine bathed the rubble, casting leering, dancing shadows in the night. He held his breath. Something suddenly growled in the blackness and ran over his legs and into the streets. A cat. A living cat. Taylor could scarcely believe it. He hadn't seen a cat—

It made it maybe halfway across the pavement when that crimson electric eye found it and a pulsing beam touched the cat. It froze up and teetered over, shattering. Taylor slipped through the wreckage and out of a cavernous hole in the wall. He was in an alley. He traveled down its length. It was L-shaped and veered off to the left. He darted down there and hid behind an overturned dumpster.

The alley suddenly lit up with an eerie, ethereal glow. It was ghostly and flickering. He waited. He had never seen anything like this before. What did it mean? His heart threatened to pound from his chest and cold sweat trickled down his spine. He heard that noise again: the one he'd heard in the subway tunnel. That heavy, cumbersome dragging sound. It was a dry, crackling noise like leaves crunching and static electricity arcing from blankets. It got closer and closer and louder. His skin was crawling and a tingling hole had opened up inside him.

Because he knew.

He suddenly knew.

He'd never seen a Stygan. He didn't think anyone ever had. No one that lived to tell the tale.

He peered from behind the dumpster to where the alley angled off. Against the frost-veined brick wall, that weird shimmering light played and pulsed and…a huge and gruesome shadow was thrown, swollen to nightmare proportions by the glow. Taylor saw a creeping, slithering mass of waving appendages and snaking limbs. Too much motion, too many things moving and coiling at the same time. He heard a strange, wet mewling sound.

He was cold and hot, his body thrumming with pure, animal terror. Because that dreadful and discordant mewling was the Stygan's voice.

Taylor screamed.

It was calling him by name.

§

An hour later, he was back in his hideout, his crib.

He dozed and woke alternately, covered in an icy sweat. He shivered with fever, his dreams dark and menacing. Finally, true sleep came and it locked him down. In his little basement apartment in the cellar of a ruined building, he slept amidst the trappings of survival and urban guerilla warfare. Tangled in black and forbidding shadow, a grim frost fell over him, wrapped him up tight and soundless like a winding sheet.

His eyes opened just before dawn.

He was not alone.

He knew that the moment consciousness flooded into his brain. He had been living by instinct, living like an animal for too long not to sense the invasion of his burrow. He came awake with the .357 Smith he kept under his pillow. He saw shadows upon shadows knotted and snarled together like jungle vines and creepers and leafage.

There was an escape route behind him. A passage that led into the sewers and to freedom.

He saw a form in the darkness, heard it breathing. The eyes glistened. "You don't need the gun," it said. "Put it away."

He went white with fear: it was his wife's voice. *Barbara*. She had been dead these many months, frozen like an icicle and, like one, shattered. And now she was back, resurrected, it would seem, via Stygan technology.

He made a dash and clicked on the battery-powered light. Their kind didn't like the light. And true to form, she shrieked and hissed, covering her ashen face with long, pale fingers. She made a hissing sound and then seemed to control herself. "Please, Charles, turn off the light. Turn it off."

And he wanted to, it was blinding.

"You've come for me," he said. A statement. "They sent you."

Between the chill shafts of her fingers, her eyes were red neon bulbs. "It was time."

And he knew it was. She had not come alone—he could hear others outside, a ghastly knot of them trembling beyond the doorway. He thought he heard others creeping up his escape passage. They sounded like snakes gliding over stone. They had him. They were making it easy on him by letting Barbara—or the thing that wore her face—take him.

It was the most he could hope for.

He dropped the gun. So tired, so broken, so defeated. But the thought of those glacial fingers bleeding the warmth from him was unthinkable. He brought out his knife and, grinning, slashed his wrists open. But there was no blood, just thick, translucent green syrup. It hung from his gashed wrists like tree sap.

"Even me," he said, his world spinning into fragments. "Even me."

Barbara offered him a mannequin's smile. Nothing more.

The war was over. And had been for some time.

Weird House

a specialty horror press
Order from **weirdhousepress.com**

ALIEN HORRORS

TIM CURRAN

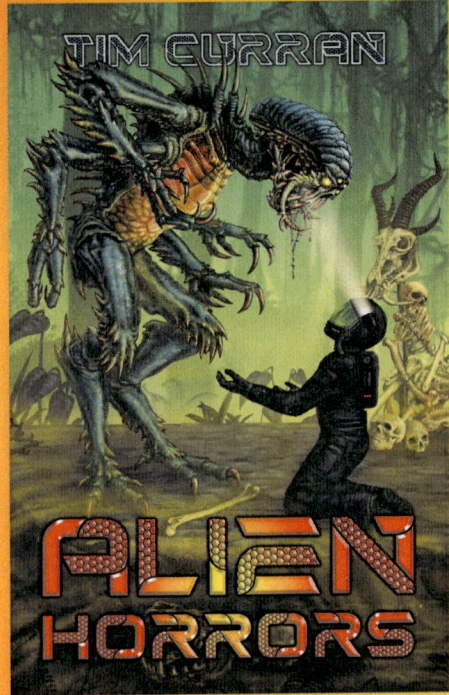

In the deepest, darkest depths of space, the stars are cold, malevolent eyes looking across a vast graveyard of the unknown, the unnamable, and the undead. Here the planets are tombs and the moons haunted catacombs. And here are extraterrestrial nightmares beyond imagining.

> There is no benevolent first contact.
> No utopian worlds.
> Only alien horrors.

Flypaper - An expeditionary team is trapped inside an alien machine that offers them anything they want at a terrible price.

City of Frozen Shadows - The last living man on Earth hides in a gutted city, hunted by alien exterminators.

The Black Ocean - Astronauts adrift in a misty alien ocean are attacked by a gigantic predator.

Charnel World - Mercenaries track the most lethal life form in the galaxy in the green hell of the planet Xenos.

Migration - A mining camp is directly in the path of a migrating alien hive.

Stowaway - The crew of a starship is stalked by a shapeshifting alien bloodsucker.

PRAISE FOR TIM CURRAN

"Tim Curran is dynamite! Visceral, violent, and disturbing!"
- Brian Keene, author of *Castaways* and *Dark Hollow*

"Curran shows his talent for creating actual frightening scenes that can linger long after reading them. If you let them. And you should. It is why we read horror after all, isn't it?" – **Darkness Dwells**

"Take down the name Tim Curran, you are going to be hearing a lot about him in the coming years." - **Scaryminds**

Signed trade paperback editions available on the Weird House Press site!
For a 10% Discount code on your next weirdhousepress.com order use code: THANKYOU
Trade Paperback and eBook editions at Amazon.com

An Interview With Tim Curran

WEIRD HOUSE: Tell us a bit about your writing process and how you approach each session. Do you have any pre-writing rituals or a process you use to get ready?

TIM CURRAN: I have no set ritual. I try to do the Hemingway thing and leave off in the middle of something so I have a place to start. And I make basic, very basic, notes so I have some direction. But other than that I approach it in a very practical manner—sit down and get that first sentence done which leads into the first paragraph. And that's the most important one because it sets mood and pace. If you get that right, the rest usually flows pretty good. There's one big mistake I made in the past and that was to over-analyze and over-think what I was going to do. It made me second-guess myself, start and stop, try a different project, looking for something I never find. Thinking and analyzing is great, but you should have that done before you write. When you sit down to write, you should fly by instinct.

WH: As an acclaimed veteran author, how does the reality of life as a writer compare to the dream you had in mind when you first started out?

TC: It's nowhere as easy as I thought it would be! And I don't mean the writing, because that's the fun part. There's all these tedious things you have to do that you never consider—copyediting, for example. Reading the same damn thing again and again. I'm not sure, knowing what I know now, if I would have even attempted any of this. It can be frustrating. It can make you angry and fill you with self-doubt. But for all that, when you get something right and people respond and love what you did or you get a movie or TV offer or an option, it feels really good.

WH: What are the keys to creating an effective writing space, in your opinion?

TC: It's good to have a room to lock yourself away in, so you can concentrate. I do my best stuff when I can do that. I like to be surrounded by my books and collections of junk. And I need quiet. I know other people play music and what not, but I can't do that. I think your best space will have a door that closes out the world and no windows. Nothing to distract you. Back in '90s when I first started writing seriously, I wrote on this big, clunky Panasonic word processor. I thought it was great, but it was pretty primitive by today's standards. Still, there was no internet so you didn't have to worry about distracting yourself with cat videos on YouTube or funny memes on Facebook.

WH: I notice a fair amount of Nightmare Before Christmas toys in your office. What's your favorite song from the film?

TC: "Kidnap the Sandy Claws"! Love that one. Of course, I love Oogie Boogie's song.

WH: There are some horror comics on your shelves. What are your favorite comics and graphic novels?

TC: This is an area I wish I was much better read in. I don't know a lot of the current stuff, which is something I'm going to change. As a kid back in '70s, I read a lot of Marvel horror comics like *Tomb of Dracula, Monster of Frankenstein, Weird War Tales* and a lot of the anthology comics Marvel put out, which were seriously watered-down versions of their 1950s comics. But I didn't know that. I read *Creepy* and *Eerie*, of course, the Skywald magazines, and lots of the stuff from Eerie Publications—*Tales from the Tomb, Witches Tales, Tales of Voodoo*, all that gory, fun stuff. I didn't realize they were mostly re-drawn from 1950s horror comics. Then one day I had an epiphany of sorts. I was walking home from school and there was a yard sale. I looked around and found a box of battered 1950s pre-code horror books (two bucks for like thirty books!). I didn't know that's what they were

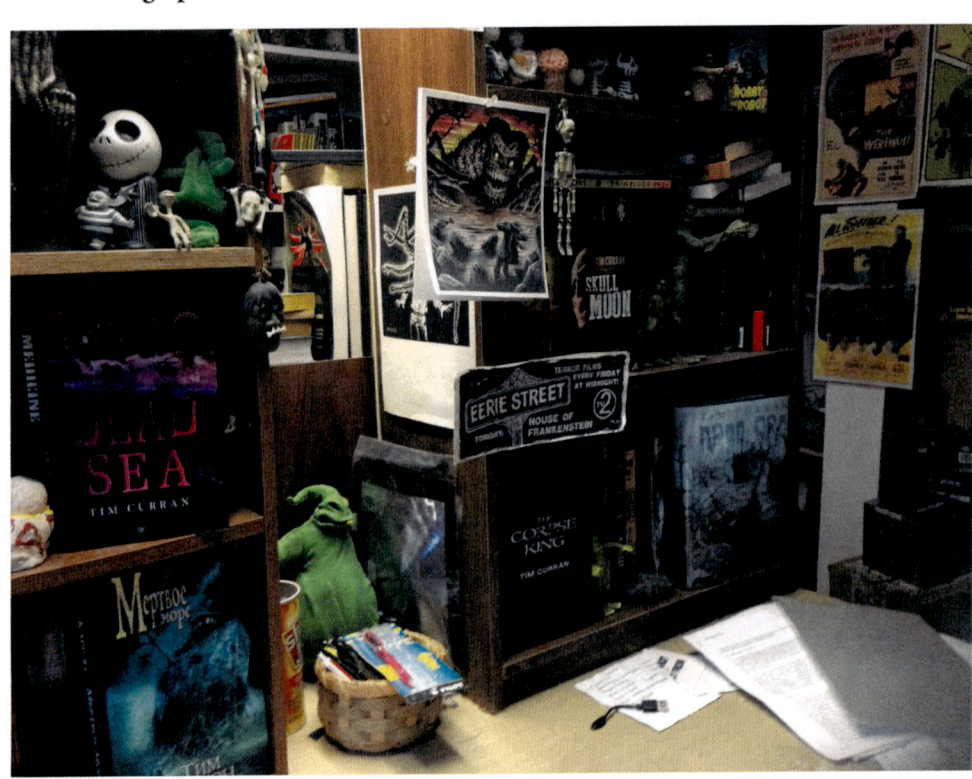

at the time, but I loved them and it made me realize how weak the contemporary Marvel and DC stuff was. Later, I discovered the EC books which are incredible, of course. I bought the hardcover, slipcased sets from Russ Cochran. When I think back now, I'd have to say I was just as much influenced by guys like Graham Ingels, Rudy Palais, and Dick Ayers as I was Lovecraft, King, and William Hope Hodgson.

WH: Do you keep all of your books in your writing room or just books you find particularly inspirational or relevant to your work/process?

TC: I keep everything here. I want easy access to books I'm using for research, my own stuff, and things by other authors if I need inspiration. I love the stacks crowding in on me.

WH: What's your favorite piece of art, model, or toy in your writing space, and what does it mean to you?

TC: Hmm. I like all my stuff, even though my wife thinks it's junk I should get rid of. I have two great statues from the *Nightmares of H.P. Lovecraft* series—Cthulhu and Dagon. I've got lots of old Aurora monster models which I love, particularly the Monster Scenes kits. But if I had to pick one thing it would be this little green rubber alien called Callisto from the Major Matt Mason toys of the

1960s. I had it when I was in Kindergarten. I carried it everywhere with me. The one I have now I bought off Ebay. The original is long gone. But it means a lot to me. It instantly connects me with my childhood.

Another question: I noted you have a picture of Vincent Price from *Witchfinder General*. Is Vincent Price one of your favorite horror actors, and which Vincent Price movie do you like the most?"

I love Price. I particularly love his Poe films he did with Corman. I can't think of any actor that epitomizes Poe better than him. He just works perfectly and naturally within that framework. As a fan of folk horror like *The Wicker Man* and *The Witch…*or is it *The VVitch?*, I love *Witchfinder General* because although it might not be 100% accurate with its depiction of Matthew Hopkins, historically it's dead-on. The intolerance, the religious mania, the sadism and brutality of the witch hunts is extremely realistic and accurate. The only quibble I have with Vincent Price is that he should have been in *Blood on Satan's Claw*. What were they thinking when they didn't cast him?

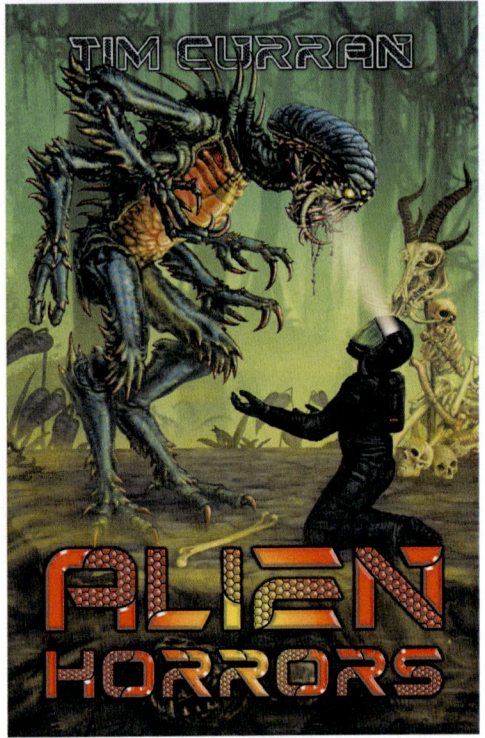

WH: You have a phenomenal collection published by Weird House called *Alien Horrors*. What are some of your favorite malevolent aliens from books, movies, comics, etc…? What about them stands out to you?

TC: I like all the standard ones from *Predator* to the Xenomorphs from the *Alien* series, *The Thing* and all that, but my particular favorites are the Martians from *Quatermass and the Pit*. Nigel Kneale really created true SF-horror with that one by explaining ghosts, religious symbolism, and occult phenomena as advanced alien technology that seemed supernatural to our less than enlightened ancestors. As much as I love stuff like *Galaxy of Terror* and *Forbidden World*, Kneale's story is thinking man's SF-horror. Lovecraft's *The Colour Out of Space* and *At the Mountains of Madness* are incredible examples of good dark science fiction. I also liked David Gerrold's Chtorr books. Cool alien monsters. But *Invasion of the Body Snatchers* is still the scariest movie, hands down (although I am a heretic in that I prefer the 1978 version). The paranoia of that one is much, much more disturbing that the paranoia of *The Thing*.

WH: Sci-fi and horror often blend seamlessly together, from the works of Shelley and Lovecraft to films like *Alien*, *Event Horizon*, and *US*. Why do you think the two genres work so well together?

WEIRD HOUSE MAGAZINE   18

TC: I think it's because of the science element. Most of us find the idea of ghosts and spooks and spirits to be more than a little silly. Even though I love that stuff, I know it's fantasy. Those things are not part of the real world. Aliens and science gone wrong are remotely feasible. You tell yourself that there could not possibly be anything like Predator or Alien or the shapeshifter from *The Thing*...but there's always a door part way open in your mind that wonders. Science-fiction horror perfectly encapsulates our fears of the unknown, the dark, strangers, and the primal terrors of nature. Call me cynical, but I rather doubt there'll ever be a situation like *Star Trek*, where this federation of aliens work together towards the common good. But an advanced alien lifeform that sees us as prey or sport? Yes, why not? How do we treat the lower lifeforms on our planet? With compassion and respect? Hell no, we hunt them and kill them wantonly. And the ones we don't, we manufacture into food.

WH: What is more important with science fiction you, creating a scientifically feasible scenario or evoking a sense of atmosphere and wonder?

TC: The latter, definitely the latter. Science works as a backdrop (most of it very theoretical) and helps to explain the mechanics of things, but atmosphere, mood, and wonder are what bring the uneasiness and fear.

WH: You are known for extreme horror. What attracts you to that style?

TC: You know, I never really considered myself an extreme horror writer in the way that Jack Ketchum or Edward Lee might be, but I understand why people would think so. It's my imagination. The imagery I see in my head when I'm writing is very detailed, very organic, and, yes, very wet in many cases. Once it pops into my head, I can't unsee it so it gets written down. Better on paper than in my dreams.

WH: You are publishing another collection with Weird House Press, titled, *Horrors of War*. Can you tell us a little bit about it?

TC: Ah, that is going to be a very, very cool book. My love of war-horror goes back to my childhood reading *Weird War Tales* and continues on to the present with my love of historical wars. Awful, inhuman, nasty things happen during wars. They represent mankind at his lowest possible ebb. Once you strip away the political correctness, patriotism, and flag-waving, what you have is sheer despair, ugliness, and depravity—the perfect background for a horror story. This collection reprints some of my favorites I published in small press magazines and books, along with some new ones. It covers warfare from the days of Genghis Khan through Napoleon, World War One to Vietnam and the Iraq War. A real labor of love for me and the artwork Brad Moore is creating for it is just unbelievable. I'm very stoked by this!

WH: Thanks so much for your time, Tim. It was fantastic getting to talk with you and see a little bit of your process and workspace! On behalf of everyone at Weird House it has been a pleasure to work with you on *ALIEN HORRORS*. We look forward to seeing what you have store in the future.

Poetry

BY
Ann K. Schwader

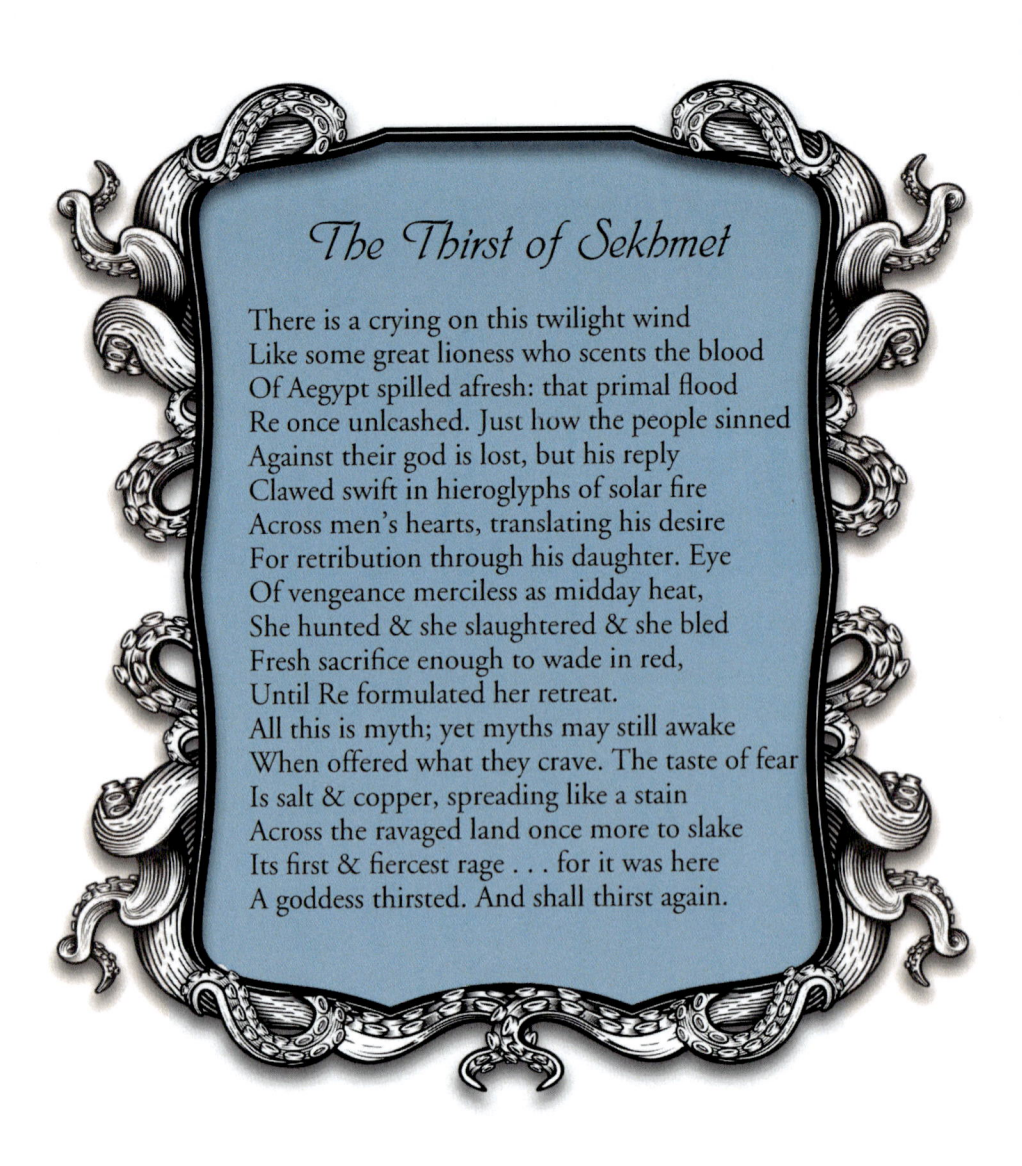

The Thirst of Sekhmet

There is a crying on this twilight wind
Like some great lioness who scents the blood
Of Aegypt spilled afresh: that primal flood
Re once unleashed. Just how the people sinned
Against their god is lost, but his reply
Clawed swift in hieroglyphs of solar fire
Across men's hearts, translating his desire
For retribution through his daughter. Eye
Of vengeance merciless as midday heat,
She hunted & she slaughtered & she bled
Fresh sacrifice enough to wade in red,
Until Re formulated her retreat.
All this is myth; yet myths may still awake
When offered what they crave. The taste of fear
Is salt & copper, spreading like a stain
Across the ravaged land once more to slake
Its first & fiercest rage . . . for it was here
A goddess thirsted. And shall thirst again.

The City in the Sands

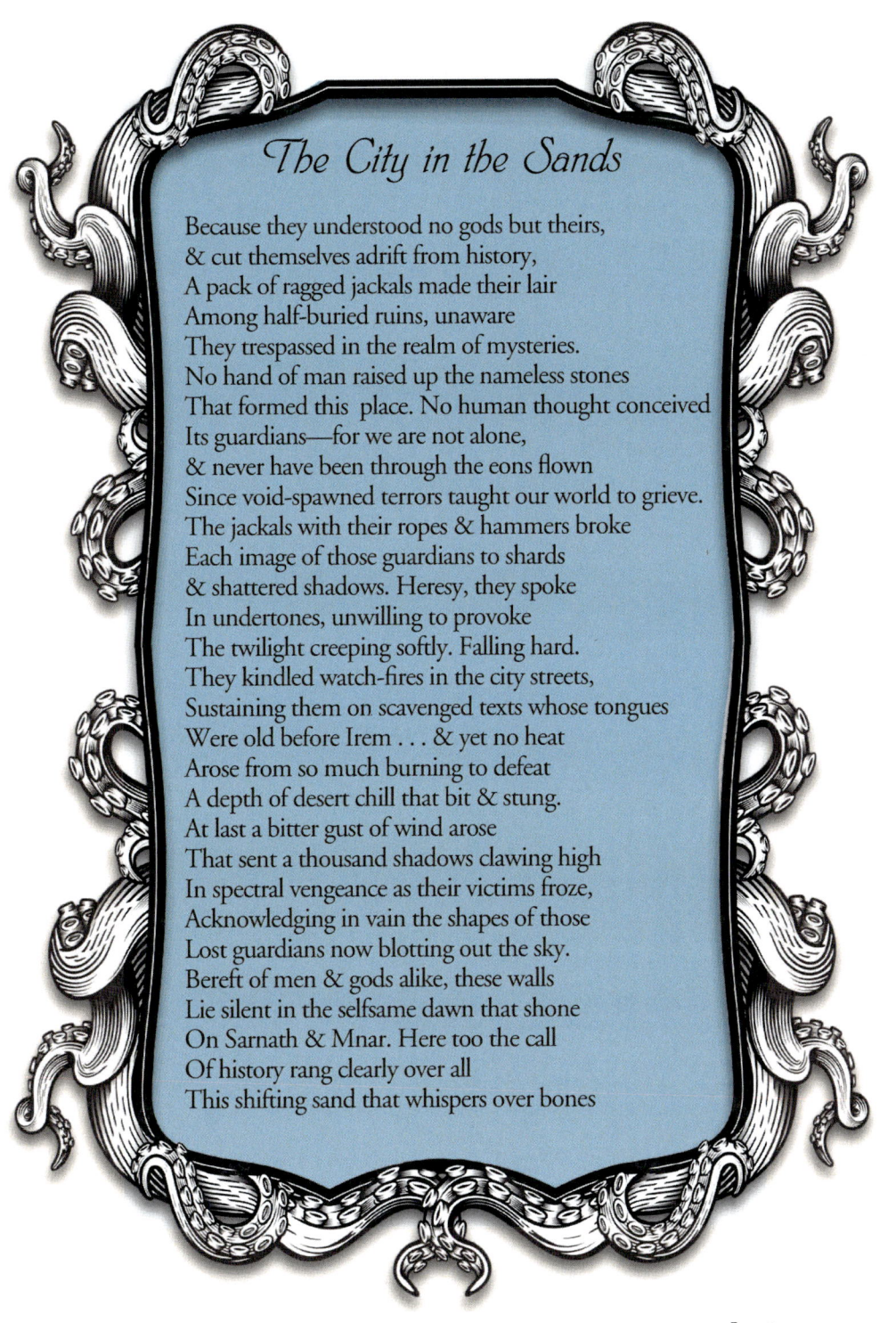

Because they understood no gods but theirs,
& cut themselves adrift from history,
A pack of ragged jackals made their lair
Among half-buried ruins, unaware
They trespassed in the realm of mysteries.
No hand of man raised up the nameless stones
That formed this place. No human thought conceived
Its guardians—for we are not alone,
& never have been through the eons flown
Since void-spawned terrors taught our world to grieve.
The jackals with their ropes & hammers broke
Each image of those guardians to shards
& shattered shadows. Heresy, they spoke
In undertones, unwilling to provoke
The twilight creeping softly. Falling hard.
They kindled watch-fires in the city streets,
Sustaining them on scavenged texts whose tongues
Were old before Irem . . . & yet no heat
Arose from so much burning to defeat
A depth of desert chill that bit & stung.
At last a bitter gust of wind arose
That sent a thousand shadows clawing high
In spectral vengeance as their victims froze,
Acknowledging in vain the shapes of those
Lost guardians now blotting out the sky.
Bereft of men & gods alike, these walls
Lie silent in the selfsame dawn that shone
On Sarnath & Mnar. Here too the call
Of history rang clearly over all
This shifting sand that whispers over bones

In Our Last Darkness

In our last darkness, the stars are lonely
as air unfettered by exhalations
of grieved meat seeking a clean & vacant
grave. In vain. No aspiring survivors
rewriting the cosmos: mythology
made campfire tales for banishing shadows
from shattered minds. No final scientists
parroting some equation that promised—
maybe—alien civilizations
avid to save us. No solitary
gazer's failing vision. Just innocent
violent furnaces scattered across
the clarity of post-apocalypse
midnight, shimmering only for themselves.

Weird House

a specialty horror press
Order from **weirdhousepress.com**

Unquiet Stars
poems by Ann K. Schwader

*Stout chains are strung at sunset to deny
all possibility of passage to
oblivion. On nights when only stars
illuminate our firmament, the sky
inside reveals a weirdly silvered view:
the moon this gate encloses is not ours.*

from "The Moon-Gate"

The ninth collection from Rhysling Award-winning speculative poet Ann K. Schwader. These poems of somber brilliance are equally magisterial as metrical formalism or as free verse. Complex and hypnotic, Schwader's work leads us down—or out—into ancient darknesses that touch us where we live.

PRAISE FOR *UNQUIET STARS*

"Ann K. Schwader is unquestionably one of the leading weird poets of our time. This new collection highlights the many virtues of her work: the meticulous crafting of every line, phrase, and word; a sense of the cosmic that brings Lovecraft and Clark Ashton Smith to mind; a deep understanding of the terror inherent in history and topography; and an enviable metrical versatility, which here includes even a few striking prose vignettes. No devotee of the weird will want to do without this scintillating volume."

—S. T. Joshi, editor of *Spectral Realms*

Purchase the beautifully designed hardcover at weirdhousepress.com
For a 10% Discount code on your next weirdhousepress.com order use code: **THANKYOU**

Trade paperback and ebook editions at Amazon.com

What I Look for in Weird Poetry

by F. J. Bergmann

Poetry is by its nature shorter and usually less complex (or complete) than fiction. It's been said that a novel is a way to try someone's life on for size; poetry is perhaps a way of trying on a feeling: of taking a single instance or event and expanding, or even better, altering, its effect to impact—and, perhaps, alter in return—the reader's perceptions, ideally in a way they would never have imagined on their own. I can't explain why I enjoy poetry so much—good poetry, that is; bad poetry is even more painful than bad fiction—except to say that tastes vary, and there exist poems for anyone that are worth discovering. Keep dipping into poems, even if you think you don't like poetry, and one day you will find a poem that will (metaphorically only, I hope) grab you by the throat and slam you against the wall.

I am not fond of poetry that attempts to stuff a saga that would be best as a short story or novel into a single poem—even less so when a lot of filler is needed to achieve uninteresting rhymes, and meter is abandoned. Nor am I fond of archaisms; e.g., 'twas and the like—a period effect, when required, can be achieved without resorting to such devices. But I adore and admire formalist poetry when done well—and Ann K. Schwader, whose book *Unquiet Stars* Weird House published in 2021 and which is nominated for the Science Fiction & Fantasy Association's Elgin Award—is one of the foremost practitioners of formalism in speculative-genre poetry. From "Apocalypse Swap":

. . . . . . Now we watch a planet trashed
& drowning in Antarctica's decay
depopulate—too slowly—in its shroud
of satellites. How many years afraid
before whatever exit we've endowed
our future with? I miss that mushroom cloud.

Poetry uses a more focused lens, allowing intense concentration that might be distracting as part of a longer prose work. Poetry also involves layers of meaning, nuance and subtext. A poem about a thing, if successful, is always about something more than just its ostensible topic, or uses one portrayal to illustrate and connect with another.

I'm enamored of poems masquerading as other forms of writing: letters, lists, instruction manuals … anything can become a poem! And any*one* can become a poem; I also have a weakness for persona poems, where the poem is in the first-person voice of someone other than the actual speaker, just like fiction written in the first person. Not necessarily the first person singular, either; from "In SETI Silence:

The Drake Equation failed us. Once we thought
belief might be enough: just listen hard
& cross your fingers. Easy. We forgot
how fragile intellect gets, battle-scarred
by every little cataclysm. . . . .

It's almost impossible to write good poetry without having a singular affection for words. Unnecessarily using sesquipedalia is annoying, but having an unusual vocabulary at one's beck and call, to be able to deliberately summon the perfect word when needed, characterizes excellent poetry. From his collection *Carpe Noctem* (Weird House Press, 2020), Robert Borski's "Kisses in the Night":

> . . . . *lacked both mariposal*
> *grace and the scent of aftershave, and was*
> *absolutely no protection from bad dreams—*
> *the slowly coagulating cocoon of blood*
> *barely hinting of metamorphoses*
> *to come.*

And, of course, here at Weird House Press, the key work is *weird*. Weirdness in poetry can range from work that only suggests something mildly outré or just a bit off from the tedium of normalcy (though what is normal anymore, in the wake of the last two years?) to full-blown speculative work that is overtly science-fictional, fantastical, or supernaturally horrific. I love the full range of poetic weirdness, ominous beginnings—from Robert Borski's "Gavage":

> *Small matter that the clipped wings*
> *have grown back; at this stage*
> *in the fattening process the beast*
> *is too big to lift itself off the ground,*
> *let alone fit through the doors*
> *of the royal stable.*
> *Moreover, gelding has further*
> *dociled the beast.* . . . .

—to stunning terminations, as in Ann K. Schwader's "Stranger Tides":

> *It falls to dreamers in their fevered nights*
> *beyond the reach of science to perceive*
> *what light & time conceal. What shadowed forms*
> *we have no names for, only myths that warn*
> *against the innocent who still believe*
> *that knowledge equals wisdom equals light.*

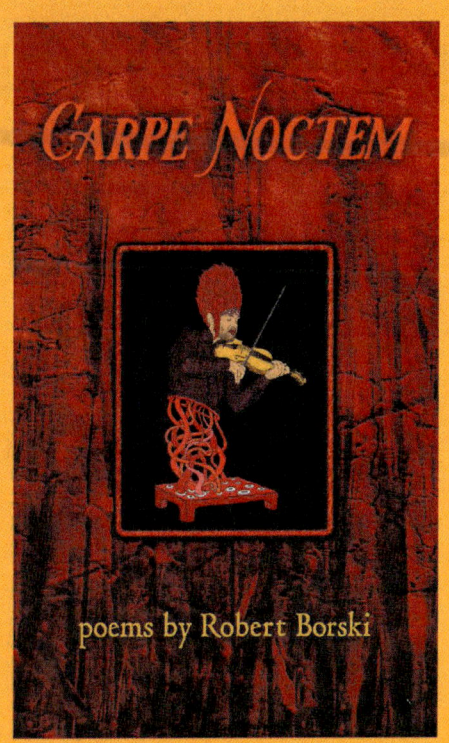

Robert Borski's weird poetry spans the lexicon of horror tropes—and then some. From the horribly funny to the truly nasty, these poems are entertaining, above all. When you open *Carpe Noctem*, you're in the hands … or the dripping claws … of a master of the genre.

… sometimes, Borski's poetry is just heart-stopping in its beauty and intelligence.
—Joselle Vanderhooft

… Borski has the skill to make something new and make us like it.
—David C. Kopaska-Merkel

One of genre poetry's greatest modern writers … A superior collection, but don't say I didn't warn you.…
—Denise Dumars

Freshest Catch

by Carol Gyzander

Muriel leaned against a post on the ferry dock in Old Harbor, barefoot, and smiled as she caught the aroma of fish. She'd been keeping an eye on this new Block Island Fish Market that had reopened near where one had been a half-century before. The young woman looked up and down the tented stalls across the parking lot, squinting her blue eyes against the bright mid-afternoon sun that made the fish scale pattern on her bathing suit shimmer as she moved. The slight breeze blew her red hair into her face, and she pushed it aside with a brisk gesture. *Damn this hair.*

Business was picking up again, now that lunch was over and one of the mid-afternoon ferries from Narragansett had come in. Rich tourists, wearing seersucker shorts embroidered with little red lobsters, made their way up and down the short row of booths, looking for something delicious for that night's dinner. After all, since they were out on an island at the edge of the Atlantic, halfway between Long Island and Cape Cod, shouldn't they eat fish?

Most of the chefs and restauranteurs had already done their shopping early that morning when the fishermen arrived and unloaded their catch fresh off the boat; this gave them time to decide the menu of the day. The prices were higher in the afternoon for the tourists, and it was worth the fishermen's time—or the time of their families—to keep the booths open so that the tourists could shop for dinner as they arrived on the ferry.

The salespeople at the closest booths occasionally gave her a side-eye glance, hardly ever looking directly at her. *They're all doing a good job of selling only the right kind of fish. The plentiful ones. Of course, I wouldn't have to shop here to get them.* She smiled at one of them and they looked away.

A chubby couple stalking from booth to booth caught her attention. In their 60s, their clothing reeked of money—as did their attitude. The man's midriff paunch was stuffed into a pair of expensive-looking Madras plaid shorts, and he wore what she could only imagine was a designer take on a Hawaiian shirt, untucked over the shorts, with a salmon-colored sweater tied around his neck by the sleeves. The boat shoes had likely never seen the surface of a boat. His hair was carefully combed and greased down so that it looked like he had more hair than he really did.

I hope he put on suntan lotion or else his scalp will be totally burned by the end of the day. On the other hand, what do I care?

His wife had curls of perfectly colored brown hair, starched in a symmetrical bob under a big straw sun hat that threatened to blow away at every breeze. Her stocky legs were encased in navy Bermuda shorts embroidered with little sailboats, under a jaunty nautical-striped tunic that gave her about the same bulbous silhouette as her husband. She wore some of those awful designer sandals, the kind with a big flower on the front that looked like they offered no arch support or protection for the woman's feet at all.

Muriel looked at her own bare feet and shrugged.

The tourist woman leaned over the meager display of fish that remained at that hour, pulling her head away and wrinkling her nose.

What kind of person shops for fish but turns her nose up in disgust when she smells fish? Muriel rolled her eyes.

The woman held her head far back with a finger under her nose and said a few words to the salesperson, who shrugged and gestured at the fish in front of her. The woman made a tsking noise and turned away abruptly, heading to the next booth without even thanking the salesperson. Her husband followed along meekly behind her.

Well. Clear to see who wears the preppie designer pants in that family.

The salesclerk noticed her watching and actually met her gaze for a moment. Muriel gestured at the couple with her chin and rolled her eyes, and the young woman snorted but then immediately stifled her reaction as she turned to the next customers approaching her booth. Muriel grinned anyway.

The haughty couple approached the next stall, where the selection was met with equal disapproval. Muriel watched as the couple marched up and down past every display booth, the woman clearly getting more and more irate that she wasn't finding what she was looking for.

Muriel approached the salesclerk who had met her gaze, waiting until she had completed the sale to her customers. "What is she looking for?"

The clerk looked up, and her eyes grew wide as she saw Muriel standing before her. "Um, you won't believe it, but she's demanding someone get her some Atlantic bluefin tuna."

Muriel's mouth dropped open despite her usual detachment. "Are you serious?"

The salesclerk shrugged. "I tried to tell her it's an endangered fish. That nobody's allowed to catch them, even though we are on the edge of their territory right now. They're so scarce. My dad would kill me if I even asked him to come back with one of those."

"My Uncle Cal would kill me, too." Muriel smiled a small smile to herself, as the young woman just nodded. *Seriously, she has no idea.* "Well, I hope you sell the rest of your fish soon so that you get to go inside where it's cool." The clerk flashed her a smile and turned to the next customer.

Muriel walked down the row of stalls, trailing the rich couple. Several shop clerks noticed her following them and nodded or inclined their heads in her direction, solemnly, then looked away. She came up behind the chubby pair, now at the final booth in the row, and quietly listened to the woman for a moment.

"I swear, I've never had such terrible service! Nobody has anything interesting at all. How am I supposed to have a dinner party for all my friends, if all you people have is regular old fish that I could get at the grocery store?"

The fish seller shrugged. "I'm sorry, ma'am. We have the freshest fish on the island, just caught early this morning. It's all wonderful and delicious. Much better than you would get on the mainland. Can I show you the—"

"No, you may *not*. I have seen all these same fish at every booth. What I'm looking for is—"

"Something special?" Muriel interrupted her tirade.

The chubby woman turned. Although they were both about the same height, the woman had her head thrown so far back by now that Muriel could see up her nose.

Muriel spoke quietly. "So, you're looking for something special, I understand? Perhaps something to … impress your friends?"

The haughty woman's eyes grew round as saucers for a moment, then she blinked quickly. "Of course. I am known for hosting an amazing dinner party. And now, we have a group here at one of the grandest houses on Block Island, but I can't find anything interesting to offer them."

"I see. Perhaps I can help you out. My family has some, shall we say, unusual contacts in the fishing industry." Muriel even made herself wink at the woman and gave a slight smile. "If you know what I mean."

The woman reached out and grasped her forearm. It was all Muriel could do to keep from pulling back, but she endured the contact of the warm, fleshy hand on her skin.

"Oh, my dear, you don't know how much that would mean to me! I mean, I have a lot of social standing and my reputation is on the line here. I need to have something *special* tonight."

"I see. And what exactly do you have in mind?"

"Well, I've heard so much about Atlantic bluefish tuna. It's supposed to be"—she leaned forward and whispered—"delicious."

You bitch. Muriel nodded. "I see why you've been having trouble here. These fishermen offer the fish that are plentiful and are legal to catch and sell because they don't impact the environment as much. They're not endangered. But the Atlantic bluefish tuna …"

She made herself lean in as well as she pulled her cell phone from her waist pouch and thumbed through the pictures. "You understand that they are quite rare. It's not just anyone who could get them for you. They live a long time, but they don't have many offspring anymore."

She showed the couple a picture of a huge, muscular fish with silvery-blue scales and recessed eyes. "This one is ten feet long."

"Exactly!" said the rich woman. "I just *knew* someone would understand. That would make such a special dinner. Don't you think?"

Muriel nodded. "Oh, it absolutely would. There's no doubt about that." She leaned back, carefully removing her arm from the pudgy hand holding it, and made a show of rubbing her chin for a minute. She looked around. "You were going to cook it yourself? Because, you know, it takes a certain skill to do it right."

"Oh, I'm sure that George here could do it. He grills everything for us. Hamburgers, chicken. Hot dogs. Wears the cutest Gucci apron."

Muriel turned and looked at George, who shrugged without saying anything.

"Yeah …" Muriel drew the word out. "You know, this is more complicated than adding mayo to Chicken of the Sea. Look, I have an idea. If you really want to wow your crowd, why don't you have them come for a special dinner at the fish market? Nobody is here at night, and we could have a whole elegant feast prepared for you by my family, who knows fish better than anyone here. We'll pull out all the stops."

At this, the rich woman's eyes were as large as saucers. "Oh, my, that's something that my friend Courtney would *never* have available. That sounds like *just* the thing I want to do. Don't you think, George?"

The man with her, who was clearly going to bankroll the entire endeavor, merely smiled and nodded. "Whatever you say, dear."

"All right." Muriel allowed herself a small smile of satisfaction. *This will indeed be just the thing for her.* "How many of you are there and where are you staying now?"

"Oh, there are eight of us altogether." The woman waved a hand vaguely toward the north. "We are staying at the biggest house on Mansion Boulevard that overlooks the Atlantic. It's such a beautiful house. I was so lucky that we were able to get it for our group of friends because they've never been anywhere like that before, you see, and—"

"Yes. Eight people. We'll have hors d'oeuvres and a beautiful dinner, and you won't have to do a thing. I promise it will be a night for everyone to remember. Look over there." Muriel gestured to a wide boathouse sitting low over the water at the end of the charter fishing boat dock, the open doorway of which allowed boats to pull in directly from the water.

"My family has owned the boathouse since before there was a fish market here the first time. Have your party here at seven o'clock tonight. Here's the address, and what the charge will be. If you give me your cell number, I can text this to you." She typed on her phone and held it up to the man, who nodded without a blink and recited his number. She forwarded the information to him.

"Great. I'm Muriel, and I will be your host for the evening. I'll bring some of my family to work the event for you." She turned to the man. "George, could you help us with this since we're so close on time? I would love to have you bring some of the wine for the dinner. I have a feeling that you two have an extensive selection of wine on hand since you clearly have such good taste. Am I right?"

The woman preened a bit, rolling her head to one side and pursing her lips as she answered for her husband. "Well, I don't mind saying that we do."

But the man perked up, now that the conversation had finally turned to something he knew about. "Of course, we do. We had several cases flown in before we even got here. I can bring some aperitif to go with the appetizers, and let's see, something fresh for the first course, and then perhaps a slightly richer wine for the dinner…" He looked from his wife to Muriel. "You did say Atlantic bluefish tuna steak, right? Perhaps a nice rich red wine …"

"It sounds like you have everything well in hand, George," Muriel assured him.

The haughty woman took control again. "All right then, it's settled. George will come early with the wine so that it can be properly chilled. I will bring the rest of the party at seven o'clock. And we will meet you at that little boathouse. You're sure it's nice enough inside?"

Oh, here we go. "It will be beautiful. Trust me. And what is your name?"

"Oh, I thought you knew. I am Ann."

Muriel tried not to flinch as the chubby woman leaned in to air kiss each cheek, wafting a cloud of perfume scent over her. *Damn. Just how bad does she smell that she needs to douse herself with that?*

"All right, I'll see you at seven. I have quite a bit to do between now and then, so I should head off." Muriel slipped out of the woman's perfume cloud and headed over to the charter dock.

She watched Ann and George as they turned and made their stately way back through the row of fish shops, noses in the air and pointedly ignoring each of the clerks in the booths as they passed. For their part, the shopkeepers watched them go by with sidelong glances from the couple to Muriel, not meeting anyone's gaze.

When Ann and George were out of sight, Muriel walked out to the end of the dock as if she were heading for one of the charter fishing boats. She looked around to ensure nobody was looking her way before diving into the water in a clean arc with no splash. She could have taken one of the boats out, but she really wanted to rinse off both the feel of the chubby woman's touch and the smell of perfume that still lingered on her red hair. So, she broke the surface and swam toward the mouth of the harbor with a strong breaststroke.

She could smell the fresh currents of the Atlantic just past the rock-covered jetty that formed the southern edge of the harbor. Once past the end of the jetty, she rolled on her back for a moment, red hair swirling around her face. Muriel stretched out her arms, buoyed by the salt water, then turned toward the open sea with a strong surge of movement.

§

Muriel and her sister, Jade, stood inside the boathouse that evening on the large dock that ran along the inside of the building. The water was open to the harbor through the opening Muriel had pointed out from the fish market. An old wooden rowboat was tied up next to a wooden ladder on the dock. They smiled at the huge painted sign on the near wall, hanging there since the old days and illuminated by lanterns on either side.

UNCLE CAL'S FISH MARKET
FRESHEST CATCH OF THE DAY!

Muriel glanced outside. The late-day sun slanted across the parking lot, the closed-up fish stalls casting shadows. All were packed away by this hour—their merchandise was sold, or the shopkeepers were out of either energy or ice.

The pair admired the beautiful table covered with a white tablecloth. It was set with silverware and lovely clear glasses that reflected the glow from the candles and the lanterns that were lit along the near wall. Even with that amount of light, the other side of the boathouse was still dim—the light didn't reach across the water. The rowboat bumped against the dock now and again, sending ripples echoing back as a wave went by in the harbor beyond.

"How do I look?" Jade ran her hands down the front of her waitress outfit—black pants, white shirt of rich fabric, and black apron. Her blonde hair was pulled back the same way as Muriel's, in a clasp adorned with pearls.

Muriel smiled. "You look lovely. It does take some getting used to, though, doesn't it? She pulled at the waistband of her own black pants. "But this is just the right look."

She heard voices approaching, and waved her arm toward the water, snapping her fingers. From the darkness on the far side came the soft sounds of ethereal classical music on a piano.

She walked to the end of the dock, coming out into the late day sunlight where the outside pathway joined the parking lot, and nodded to George who was on his second glass of wine while he was talking animatedly on his phone. He was wearing khaki slacks and a polo shirt, with the same salmon-colored sweater tied around his neck. *At least those chunky thighs look better in long pants.*

"Welcome to Café Pearl," she called to the group of seven middle-aged folks who were disembarking from the taxi van. "We have everything ready for you. Please, come in and join us."

Ann took the lead, linking arms with a slender, deeply tanned woman and speaking over her shoulder so the others coming along behind could hear her. "You see, Courtney, here it is. I have something special lined up that we won't get anywhere else! George, come along."

George terminated his call and they all followed Muriel into the dim boathouse, clumping together and pausing to blink a few moments as their eyes adjusted to the darkness.

Muriel stood with her back to the water and faced the group.

"Hello, everyone. I'm Muriel, and this is my sister, Jade." She gestured to the blonde woman at the far end of the table. "My family has joined together here to provide you with the most amazing dining experience of your lives, including a delicacy that you will not find anywhere else. Please, may we offer you an aperitif?"

Jade approached with a tray of long-stemmed glasses of sparkling white wine and offered a glass to each guest. When all were served, she retreated into the darkness at the back of the boathouse and returned in a moment with a dish of grilled shrimp and mango skewers.

"Look everyone, Jade has some delicious treats for us." Ann waved her hand to draw her crowd around her as Jade approached with the first round of hors d'oeuvres.

§

Eventually, the group moved to their seats at the table, exclaiming when the rowboat bumped against the dock now and again with a splashing noise.

The dinner progressed through several starter courses with accompanying wine selections. Somewhere between the fresh shrimp salad on endive and the Oysters Rockefeller, George answered his phone loudly, slurring his speech a bit. "Whaddya mean there's a problem with the card?"

Standing in the shadows, Muriel grinned as Ann glared daggers at him. He caught his wife's eye and pushed back from the table.

Putting his hand over the phone, he called out to the group. "Go right on ahead, everyone. Enjoy the 'spensive food. I may be a while." He lurched outside, already talking before he was out of the boathouse.

Ann gave a high-pitched laugh. "He's been working on a business deal that has been taking up all his time this vacation. I'm sure he'll be back soon." She gestured to Jade for more wine.

The group sat at the dining table in the little island of candlelight, with Ann at the head, as it grew dark outside. The wine was flowing freely, and all of the guests appeared to be relaxed and having a good time. Many were rather tipsy, lolling in their chairs and beaming at each other as they exclaimed about the delectable aroma of something being grilled over charcoal. One man pointed and laughed at the candlelight reflecting off ripples in the dark water and the echoes of splashes.

Muriel waited while Jade cleared the oyster plates and forks from the table. When there was a lull in the conversation, she stepped forward out of the shadows. "My esteemed guests, we now come to the dinner course. Your hostess, Ann, has arranged a most amazing delicacy for your enjoyment tonight. She came to the fish market this afternoon looking for Atlantic bluefin tuna. The other fisherman's booths refused to provide you with this rare treat. But Ann persevered, and because she did so, I am delighted to offer you an entrée such as you have never had before."

She beckoned toward the shadows at the back of the boathouse. A strong young man with striking green eyes approached, pushing a cart that bore a platter covered with a large silver dome. It clinked as the cart rumbled over the uneven surface of the dock. He stopped by Ann and looked around the table. Once he had all their attention, he reached forward and removed the silver dome with a flourish.

"Gentle ladies and gentlemen, you came here for tuna steak, and we have the most delectable steak selection for you."

The platter was heaped with large circular slabs, fresh off the grill with a bone in the middle of each piece. An enticing aroma filled the space.

Muriel gave a small smile as each guest leaned toward the platter with rapt attention. "Finn and Jade, would you please serve our guests?"

Finn carefully served a large grilled portion onto each dinner plate, and Jade placed them before the guests one at a time.

"It's such a shame that George is missing the main course. What can be keeping him?" the tanned woman sitting next to Ann asked her.

"Oh, Courtney, it's not like he says much anyway. He'll be along presently." Ann's gaze flitted back and forth between the beautiful, juicy offering on the platter and the appreciative looks of her guests as they received their portion. "He wouldn't want us to stop the party on his behalf. Everyone, please enjoy! It's been my pleasure to provide you with this amazing, rare delicacy."

Muriel's fist clenched for a moment until she forced herself to relax. As Jade served the last diner, Finn pulled the cart back into the shadows.

The guests all stopped chatting as they dove in to enjoy their main course. The only sounds were the clinking of cutlery on the fine plates, smacking of lips, and chewing.

Courtney cut a delicate-sized bite and placed the morsel in her mouth, holding her pinky out from the fork as she did. Ann watched her friend's every movement. She chewed and then rolled her eyes, sitting back in the chair with her hand on her chest. "Oh, Ann, this is amazing! I've never had anything like this. You are right, it was totally worth the expense."

A chorus of compliments echoed around the table as each guest enjoyed the main course.

Ann beamed and waved her hand in the air. Then she frowned. "I am surprised, though, that it has such a dense texture. I thought perhaps tuna would be, I don't know, flakier."

Muriel stood at the edge of the ring of candlelight, watching the pretentious guests consume the meal. Her voice floated from the darkness into the sounds of chewing. "Yes, ma'am, but it has a dense texture because it is from such a large creature. Think of swordfish steaks."

Just a little bit longer now.

"What was that?" A woman at the other end of the table stared out across the dark water. "I thought I saw something!"

Jade was instantly at her side, holding a wine bottle. "Ma'am, have you tried the Syrah yet?" She poured the woman a glass of wine and the woman turned from the water to try a sip, then went back to her meal.

When most of the guests had consumed a large amount of their portion, Muriel moved next to Ann. "Is everything to your satisfaction, ma'am?"

"Yes, indeed. My friends tell me that they've never had anything like this before. It's just such a shame that George couldn't be with us."

"Well, I believe that he can join us now. Would you like me to have him brought in?"

Ann stared at her with a frown. "Of course! He's my husband."

Muriel snapped her fingers, and Finn returned, pushing the cart again. This time there was no platter on it. Instead, the body of George lay on the cart, arms flopping off the sides and bouncing a bit each time the cart hit a bump.

Both of his legs were missing, sawn off at mid-thigh. The cut ends of his legs faced the group at the table, the exposed ends of the bone matching the steaks on their plates. The diners looked up and stared for a moment. One woman screamed and fainted, tipping sideways to fall upon her neighbor.

Courtney sat back in shock. "Oh, my God. George. Oh my God. Look at his legs!" She looked down at her plate, then back at the body of their host. "They cut off his legs. And that's what they grilled for our dinner!"

Her husband, seated next to her, immediately vomited all over his plate.

As two of the men started to pull back from the table, Finn moved behind them and blocked their chairs. Muriel stepped up next to Ann and gripped the pudgy woman's shoulder, holding her in her seat. Her voice rang out across the group.

"Stop! You are all complicit in this. This woman insisted upon purchasing Atlantic bluefin tuna, an endangered species that is not producing enough offspring. An intelligent creature that lives for forty years in the depths of the ocean, never bothering you or your kind. Yet they have been hunted and fished almost to extinction."

She looked around the group of white-faced, privileged, over-entitled rich people.

"You're appalled at eating a piece of your friend? That's the same way I felt when this woman asked to buy a piece of Atlantic bluefin tuna for dinner. I *know* some of them. Have known them for decades. You have no business making a meal out of an intelligent creature."

Ann started to stand, blustering as she tried to push up from the table. Muriel slammed her back down in her chair and the heavy woman crashed into the back of the seat.

Muriel stood over her. "None of you are going anywhere. None of you deserve to walk this earth when you cannot live in harmony with it. I've decided to treat you the same way that you treated what you thought was an Atlantic bluefin tuna."

A small smile played around her lips.

"I'm going to serve *you* to *my* family. Uncle Cal?"

At her words, the water next to the dock inside the boathouse roiled and splashed. Several large tentacles reached out and grabbed onto the edge of the dock, pulling a massive rust-colored body partway out of the water. A gigantic eye surveyed the scene and then focused upon Ann, as more tentacles slithered up from the depths. The eye was the size of her head. Beneath it was a huge, hooked beak of a mouth.

<*Now is the time?*>

"Yes, Uncle Cal. Now is indeed the time."

Muriel, Jade, and Finn backed away from the table.

Uncle Cal gripped the dock with one tentacle, bracing part of his huge bulk out of the water. The other seven tentacles shot out and latched onto each of the diners with suckers the size of their dinner plates. The gargantuan cephalopod ripped them out of their seats one at a time, bashing some of their heads on the table and dragging their bleeding forms into his gigantic, gaping maw. Others were lifted, still screaming and wriggling, to be enjoyed alive.

He plucked what remained of George off the cart as dessert.

When all were consumed, the huge body slipped back into the water. <*A delightful meal, my dear. Freshest Catch of the Day, for sure! Thank you so kindly for hosting the dinner party.*>

Muriel nodded, surveying the wreckage, then gestured for Jade and Finn to help as she started clearing the dishes from the table. One plate was covered with blood, either from the host's leg or one of the diners. She wiped up a fingerful and licked it off.

"Well, what do you know. Tastes like chicken."

The Lingering Terror of Silent Hill

By Robert Ottone

A foggy street. A flashlight. A pocket radio that emits static and if you're lucky, a voice carried from another place. Gloom. Creatures shifting in the gloom of a town that's seemingly been forgotten to time. Broken people. Monsters borne from our darkest fears or deepest desires.

Welcome to *Silent Hill*.

Debuting in 1999 for the original PlayStation, *Silent Hill* was everything *Resident Evil* wasn't. Whereas Capcom's survival horror title emphasized action, inventory management and a punishing save system, Konami's offering focused instead on elements of horror that resonate differently, player to player. The original game's story, where father Harry Mason searches the titular town for his missing daughter after a car accident explores a brand of horror that hadn't been focused on much in gaming to that point: the terror of being a parent.

Harry's story in that first game is rooted in the concept of protecting one's child from the forces of the outside world. It doesn't help that those forces come in the form of disturbing creatures like the "Air Screamer," "Grey Child" or even the final boss of the game itself, known as "Incubus" play with Judeo-Christian imagery, while incorporating elements of Stephen King's *The Mist* as well as interpretations of monsters from H. P. Lovecraft. My interpretation of the game's theme has always been a fear of the unknown and of protecting one's child from whatever the darkness lurks at the edge of town. But my interpretation aside, why do we connect with Harry so much in that first entry?

"He's a widower and father to an adopted daughter. That's a one-two punch to the viewer's emotions: loss and responsibility," says Todd Keisling, author of the Bram Stoker Award-nominated novel *Devil's Creek*.

"We encounter his loss and responsibility firsthand. Silent Hill is deserted and blanketed in fog, which immediately conveys Harry's sense of isolation and loneliness."

One of the most important things to keep in mind while enjoying a *Silent Hill* game is that more often than not, at least in the original four titles, the protagonist wasn't a gun-toting action hero like Chris Redfield of *Resident Evil* or the Doom Slayer from, well, *Doom*. The "heroes" in *Silent Hill* were ordinary people in extraordinary circumstances. Harry being a totally average person, an "everyman" of sorts only brings us closer and allows us to connect even further, because we can ask questions like "What would I do in this situation?" and we can then see our avatar react in a realistic way. In reality, we rely on our fight or flight instincts, and the *Silent Hill* series plays on that repeatedly.

"They say Lovecraft was scary because he left so much to the imagination and I agree with that assessment, but *Silent Hill* shows how far NOT leaving things to the imagination can get you," says Eric Peacock, host of the *Soundtracker* podcast. "The creature designs (which I think were helped by the PS1s limited power) wedge their way under your skin. Once you get your first glimpse of what's waiting for you in the fog, or the darkness, every single new area you enter makes you want to set your controller down and stop. Don't move and you'll be safe. But that's not how video games work, is it? So, you press on, and know that eventually you're going to cross paths with Pyramid Head again. A good creature design can be just as scary as anything you come up with in your imagination, especially when the game itself is pure atmosphere."

Masahiro Ito, the man who designed Pyramid Head, gave us a variety of demented nightmares to encounter in *Silent Hill 2*, the franchise entry many consider the "holy grail" of horror gaming (I'm one of those people). Just two short years after the original *Silent Hill*, the sequel would seemingly appear from the mist and deliver an experience that was a grand departure from the original title. The score, by Akira Yamaoka, relied heavily on a variety of tonalities and instruments, adding layers of emotional connective tissue via music the horrific and entrancing visuals on display.

"Thematically, what appeals to me is that the series, particularly *Silent Hill 2*, is that it cloaks themes like grief and guilt—these universal things—in horror," says Peacock. "Which is old hat (in the genre as a whole), but it was new to video game storytelling and what it was capable of at the time this series began."

The second entry's story centers around James Sunderland, who arrives in the titular town after receiving a letter from his dead wife. With that simple yet effective premise (which owes a lot to *The Twilight Zone*, *Jacob's Ladder* and perhaps surprisingly Fyodor Dostoevsky's *Crime and Punishment*), players are tasked with rediscovering familiar areas, though with altogether new presentation, thanks to the increased power of the PlayStation 2 and Xbox hardware.

While the location of the first game certainly felt like a mysteriously empty place shrouded in fog and loaded with nightmares, the town of the second game builds upon that by playing tricks on the player. Audio cues and messages in the environment help round out the unsettling and off-putting nature of the game, forcing players to mistrust everything around them. This even speaks to James' mental state as the game progresses. In an interview with IGN from 2001, artist and writer Takayoshi Sato discussed the idea of putting story first, knowing the heavy-lifting of having to establish a moody and atmospheric setting had already been accomplished by the first entry.

"So, when making *Silent Hill 2*, we already knew roughly what the environment was going to look like, so we could build the entire story before designing the game. We think that this makes the town of Silent Hill a more realistic place overall," Sato told IGN in 2001, adding "We're trying to combine horror and a dramatic story. Obviously, we want to scare the player, but we'd also like it if the player were to cry at some of the more emotional scenes."

I discovered the game in college while taking a semester off after not being able to keep my grades up in the law program I was enrolled in. I didn't want to disappoint my dad, so I moved back home and took a semester off. That meant working and playing video games. One of those games was *Silent Hill 2: Restless Dreams*, the "enhanced" edition of the title that included a special scenario exclusive to Xbox gamers. It quickly became an all-time favorite and helped me at a time where I was feeling sorry for myself all the time, unsure about my future and with limited prospects to keep me going. *Silent Hill 2: Restless Dreams* gave me the inspiration to write. To tell stories. This was a pastime I hadn't been able to enjoy since high school, and yet thanks to *Silent Hill 2* and the rabbit hole of influences I went down, I rediscovered my love for creation at the depths of one of my most sorrowful moments.

Silent Hill 2 was the first time I, personally, ever had an emotional reaction to a video game. Sure, Sephiroth killing Aeris was rough, but nothing could ever prepare me for James' journey into the depths of his own desires and heartache. His feelings were altogether too real, and in writing this article, I was happy to learn I wasn't alone.

"When the game was released in 2001, I was a freshman in college. My dorm roommate was pledging to a fraternity, so he was never around. I was alone most of the time, didn't know anyone and was too socially awkward to make new friends," says Keisling. "I'd just gone through a breakup, which kicked off a months-long period of depression. The immediate goal of finding James' wife wasn't as compelling to me for some reason, the rest of the characters were unlikable, and the overall plot was too obscure. I just didn't have the same connection to it as the first, despite the amazing graphics and sound design."

The graphics, sound design and overall story have allowed players and writers to continue to dissect the second entry more than twenty years after its release. "A lot of the obscure elements that turned me off at 18 suddenly made sense at the age of 30," says Keisling. "Given all I was going through at the time, I couldn't see how the game reflected a lot of what I was feeling, and so that connection wasn't immediately apparent. Like James, I was lost in the fog, seeking some kind of closure over a relationship gone sour."

That's perhaps the most haunting thing *Silent Hill 2* presents to us as players. A story that hinges on the interpretation of events, locations and relationships. I won't spoil the game here, but James' story must be experienced to be believed. Simply watching a Let's Play on YouTube won't do it any justice, you need to play the game yourself and really ruminate on the narrative to appreciate it. That sounds insanely pretentious, but seriously, just play it. Then sit and think about it.

It would be silly to not take a second to mention the replayability of these games. Each title offers a myriad of different endings, some leaning heavily into the absurd. "The *Silent Hill* series, for all of the dark, adult themes it touches upon, also has the funniest easter egg/alternate endings of any series, and I think that's helped it endure over the years," says Peacock. The franchise also features some of the darkest endings in gaming history with characters choosing to commit suicide, allowing their friends and loved ones to suffer horrendous fates and more.

"As I get older, the scariest thing to me is that the people who wind up in Silent Hill just aren't objectively 'good' people," says Julian Titus, host of *Nerds Without Pants*, a podcast dedicated to gaming. "That said, a lot of them are in these personal hells because of things they did that any of us could end up doing or being guilty of doing."

A particularly personal hell is exactly what awaits Heather, the protagonist of *Silent Hill 3*. Two years after the artistic triumph of *Silent Hill 2*, the third entry made its debut featuring a series first – a female protagonist. Not only was the gender of the lead different than the two previous entries, her age was as well. Where Harry and James were adult men, Heather was a teenaged girl. She wasn't your standard video game heroine like Lara Croft from *Tomb Raider* or Tifa Lockheart from *Final Fantasy 7*. Heather was a child. She wasn't dolled up like a bizarre fantasy of what a woman *should* be. She was quick-tempered. She was a normal American girl faced with a hell that no one should face.

A direct sequel to the original game, Heather finds herself squaring off with the remnants of the cult that operates in the town. While largely absent from the second game, The Order attempts to use Heather to awaken their God and purify the world through cult-y shenanigans. Truth be told, the cult aspects of the franchise has always been the least interesting part to me, but the lore of the cult makes for a fascinating read.

"At the time I found that it was refreshing to play as a female protagonist and when compared to Harry and James, her reactions to what was going on around her was more realistic as it often mirrored my own as a young woman," says Whitney Chavis, host of *Voices in the Static* and curator of the Silent Hill Historical Society website.

What makes *Silent Hill 3* such a thrilling entry is exactly that. Seeing how Heather reacts to things going on around her. She's not a brooding figure like James or a desperate father like Harry. She is simply a young woman pulled into a nightmare. In a pivotal moment in the game, after Claudia Wolf, the leader of The Order has Heather's father murdered, the teenager states her intention to return to Silent Hill, proclaiming "I don't know what kind of hell is waiting for me there, but I've got no other choice. I don't care about God or Paradise... If that's what she believes in then fine. But she won't get away with what she did. When I find her, I'll kill her myself."

It's a reaction like that that lingers with us as players. Heather functions again as an "everyman" character, reacting in a natural way. She indulges her feelings, regardless of how they may play out. We've all been pulled toward dark thoughts or toward dark actions and only through the grace of maturity and age are we able to realize that doing something rash isn't the way to go. Heather, blinded with rage, seeks revenge and we can all get on board with it. It plays a trick on us, in that we're rooting for this child to murder her way to Claudia and of course, that's what happens. *Silent Hill 3* is almost a metacommentary on gaming in general in that by featuring a female protagonist and placing her in danger, it then casts *us* as the role of her protector. We *become* Harry Mason from the first game, and when Heather's father (spoilers: Harry Mason from the first game) is murdered, she's untethered and we, like Heather are then guided purely by revenge.

It's that meta commentary that brings us to the entry that in recent years has seen a resurgence. *Silent Hill 4: The Room* doesn't even take place in the town itself, instead taking place largely in Ashfield, a small, neighboring city. *The Room* is perhaps the entry most inspired by Japanese folklore and horror, wearing its influences proudly and featuring floating, gray-skinned ghosts, terrifying conjoined twin-creatures and more. J-horror had been thriving in Japan for years by the time 2004 came around, thanks to incredible titles like *Kairo*, *Ju-On* and *Ringu*. *The Room* borrowed heavily from those works not only in tone and visual but in theme as well. *Kairo*, for example, deals with themes of loss and loneliness. *The Room*'s protagonist, Henry Townshend, is a lonely young man trapped in his apartment. His *haunted* apartment. Complete with chains on his front door with lettering scrawled in red: "Don't go out!! – Walter"

"I love the Japanese take on American horror," says horror author Anthony J. Engebretson. "It's like you wound up in hell, but hell is wearing a familiar façade."

The familiar hellish façade in this case, much like the traditionally "normal" locations of previous games in the series, seem altogether more "normal" this time around. In *Silent Hill 3*, Heather ventures to an amusement park, albeit a hellish one. Not an everyday location, for sure. In *The Room*, Henry finds himself in subway stations, the woods outside of Silent Hill, his bathroom, his kitchen, a lake. Normal places one could visit whenever they want and yet, interpreted through the Otherworldly hellscape of *Silent Hill 4: The Room*, altogether bizarre and unsettling.

"*The Room* feels like an actual nightmare in that 'you try to open a door knob but your hands don't work'-kinda' way," says horror author Tom Coombe. "The ghosts you can't kill, the way your apartment becomes more 'infected' as the game goes on, it just feels so nightmarish to me."

The game's protagonist, Henry, is a departure from previous leads in that he's not as brave or as sure of himself as Heather, not as driven as Harry and not as layered as James and yet, he still feels real. He feels like

WEIRD HOUSE MAGAZINE

a person sleepwalking through a nightmare, which I think marks this entry as a high mark for the series in that it does something dramatically different than previous entries. While those other *Silent Hill* titles feel like we're a character exploring a mystery and horror within the town, *The Room* takes us on a more personal and frightening story with dark implications for our lead and those around him.

Henry navigates the various "levels" of the nightmare with his apartment acting as a central hub of sorts. Over time, it becomes more haunted: floating heads outside his living room window, ghosts clawing their way out of his walls, windows rattle, the television turns on and loudly blasts static, entities at your door's peephole, all equally unnerving as the game goes on.

"I played this game at a time in my life when I was in a long-distance relationship and living alone, my depression still undiagnosed and unmedicated," Coombe says. "Like Henry in the game, my apartment started to feel like my whole world."

Part of the reason that *The Room* has gained in popularity and gained appreciation in the minds of longtime fans and new devotees alike surely is due in part to the current pandemic. Hell, when COVID started and New York was in lockdown, during online conferences and calls, I had my background set to Henry's haunted apartment, chained front door and all. "Our apartments and homes became our entire world then," adds Coombe. "*The Room* may have come out in the early aughts, but in that sense, it feels very modern."

Each hero in the franchise has had their own cross to bear. Harry's confusion and desperation to find his daughter. James' personal torment. Heather's dark destiny. Henry's isolation. The original four games all speak to aspects of the human condition that we can all relate to in some capacity.

Now, imagine for a moment that one could experience all of these things in one overarching narrative. Elements of all four of those games. The personal torment of the *Silent Hill 2*, the first-person isolation and dream-like atmosphere of *Silent Hill 4: The Room*, the darkness of *Silent Hill 3* and the desperation and confusion of the original *Silent Hill*.

Add all of that together and release it as a playable teaser back in 2014 and you have *P. T.* – aka: *Silent Hills*, the cancelled franchise soft-reboot created by the enigmatic and brilliant Hideo Kojima of the *Metal Gear* franchise. Starring *The Walking Dead*'s Norman Reedus and produced by Guillermo Del Toro and horror manga artist/writer Junji Ito, *P. T.*'s story is almost completely unknown but was set to feature a lead character dealing with the horrors of a murder committed in the past by either himself or his father with a reliance on a spectral tormentor named Lisa, who follows the player and can strike almost any time as the one makes their way through seemingly-endless looping hallways in a modern-looking haunted house.

"The atmosphere is incredible," says Jess, co-host of the *What's Your (Least) Favorite Scary Movie* podcast. "The looping hallway is very claustrophobic. The space itself keeps you on edge."

The demo itself garnered remarkably positive reviews for its ability to build tension, layer narrative and mystery and not give too much away. The horror elements were plentiful and the voice acting and sound design were top notch. No two playthroughs are exactly the same and that's what kept gamers coming back to go through and unravel the mystery over and over, hoping to pick up clues at every turn.

"Even if you've played it a hundred times, you'll still have a unique experience," says Trav, co-host of the *What's Your (Least) Favorite Scary Movie* podcast. "There's an air of uncertainty of what will happen next."

No two pieces of gameplay footage are exactly the same. While *P. T.* wasn't immediately revealed to be a *Silent Hill* title, those who made it through the never-ending hallways and corridors of the haunted house in the demo were eventually rewarded with an amazing in-engine cutscene showing the protagonist (Reedus) walking down the eerie and poorly-lit streets of a familiarly foggy town before the screen faded to white-gray, the title *Silent Hills* eventually emerging from the fog. This title gave fans the impression that Kojima, notorious for densely-layered narratives, was somehow playing with the idea of multiple universes within the *Silent Hill* universe. This is something we've seen in the series before, but hadn't been focused on too heavily. Unfortunately, the game was cancelled and Kojima parted ways with Konami so its likely we'll never truly know what that game could have been.

Which in a way, I enjoy. *Silent Hills* or *P. T.* functions better as a work produced in the theater of the mind. Whatever we would get at this point in time would surely not live up to whatever we'd all collectively constructed. There's a lot to take in from the world of *Silent Hill* and with the vast darkness within ourselves, we can toil away and live in the town as long as we want.

The terror that lies at the heart of *Silent Hill* will always be the terror that's within *us*. The monsters are horrifying, sure. The imagery and the locations, unsettling. But the true mark of good horror is when it tugs at us on a personal level. When we can see even the tiniest bit of ourselves in the lead character, good or bad. The characters in the *Silent Hill* franchise react how we react. They say things we might say. They feel things we might feel. *Silent* Hill pushes us to the limits of psychological horror and forces us to confront the true darkness of our id. That intense moment of panic that rises in one's chest when staring into the dark living room on your way up to bed. Walking alone at night down an empty neighborhood street. Driving down a deserted road late in the evening.

"Horror of the self will always speak to us because it reveals the demons within, the ones we try to hide from others, and sometimes from ourselves," Keisling says. "It forces us to acknowledge all the ugliness inside, what we keep hidden beneath all that fog."

That's where Silent Hill lives. Lurking in the depths. Waiting in the fog to welcome you.

Robert P. Ottone is the author of the horror collection HER INFERNAL NAME & OTHER NIGHTMARES (an honorable mention in THE BEST HORROD OF THE YEAR VOLUME 13) as well as the young adult dystopian-cosmic horror trilogy THE RISE.
He can be found at spookyhousepress.com or on twitter/Instagram (@RobertOttone)

The Gravedigger's Tale

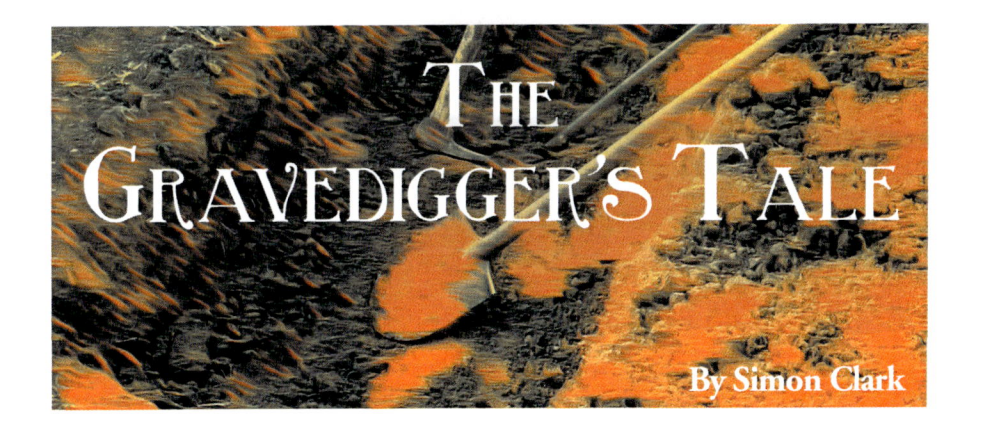

By Simon Clark

"Jesus!" exclaimed the electrician, as he levered the back off the hulking, great chest freezer. "What did you have to dig 'em back up for?"

Weathered brown, whip-lean, sixty-plus, half-smoked cigarette behind one ear, the gravedigger grinned, displaying an uneven row of yellow splinters that had once been teeth; he leaned forward, bare wrinkled elbows resting on the freezer lid.

"The new by-pass. It's going to take half the graveyard yonder, so before they lay the new road, we have to lift the blighters and plant 'em in the new municipal ground up on Pontefract Road."

Pulling a face, the electrician wiped the palms of his hands on his overalls. "There must have been some sights. Well, they've been dead years."

"Aye. First one were interred in 1836. So… most of the coffins were well rotted. Soon as you tried to lift 'em,"—he made a wet crackling sound—"they just folded—just folded like wet cardboard boxes. And everything—everything spilled out into a heap. Just imagine that." The gravedigger waited for the young man's reaction."

"Jesus." He wiped his mouth as if something small and extremely unpleasant had just buzzed into it. "You must have a strong stomach."

The gravedigger recognized the inflection in the young man's voice. Disquiet, distaste, unease. He eyed the electrician up and down. The floppy white hat, slack mouth and wide-eyed gormless look signalled, here's a lad that believes everything; every tall story that comes his way he'll swallow; the kind of lad that cropped up on every factory floor, in every shop and office, who when asked would conscientiously hurry to the foreman or stores' manager to ask for the long-wait, or jar of elbow grease, or a pair of sky-hooks. The gravedigger had been steeling himself for a dull afternoon of ten Woodbines, five cups of tea and a solo darts tournament in the cemetery store-cum-restroom. However, a faulty freezer, and Fate at her most obliging, had brought entertainment in the shape of the young electrician in his floppy white hat; someone who was, the gravedigger realized, as green as he was cabbage-looking. "I'm just brewing up. You'll want a wet when you've done."

"Oh, ta. Milk and two sugars. Trouble is with this unit, it's been too near the window. Direct sunlight makes them overheat. Shouldn't take long though." He looked round the untidy, brick-floored room. Spades, shovels, picks, rusting iron bars leaned into dusty corners. Fading graveyard plans curled away from the corrugated iron walls; at the far end stood a table cluttered with chipped mugs, cigarette boxes, empty milk cartons, and the greasy remains of a Cornish pasty. Overhead, an asbestos ceiling punctuated by dozens of tiny brown corpses—that had died and been mummified by the dry air.

"Are the others out, you know, digging?" the electrician asked conversationally.

"Oh, aye." The old man accurately tossed tea bags into two mugs. "They're working up the top-side. Look." He pointed a yellow-brown nicotine-stained finger that boasted a startlingly large black fingernail. Through a grimy, cobwebbed window two men could be seen digging in the graveyard. They hurled spades full of soil over their shoulders with cheerful abandon. "That's where they're going to plant James Hudson, the old Mayor. Top-side, you see, is where all your nobs are—doctors, solicitors, aldermen, bank managers. Bottom-side is for your working folk and paupers."

"And that's where the new road's going through." The young man returned to work, prising at cables with a screwdriver, while whistling in such a way it would make a saint curse.

"Aye... that's where they have to be dug up." The gravedigger licked his lips. 'Disinterred. Exhumed. Aye." Taking the kettle from the solitary electric ring, he limped to the freezer top, which he used as an impromptu table. There, he filled the mugs with boiling water. Then he paused. Dreamily he stared into the rising steam. "Aye, a bad business this disinterring. You see some things so bad it makes you fair poorly. You know in some of the older graves? Well, we opened coffins and found..."

"Found what?"

"We opened the coffins and found that the bodies had..." Once more his voice trailed away.

The electrician's eyes opened wide.

"Well. They'd moved."

"Moved? The bodies had moved?"

"You see, sometimes years ago, people got buried alive. Not deliberately of course. 'Spect some poor wretches were in comas so deep they were certified dead. They buried them. Course, then they woke up." He glanced at the electrician to see if he appreciated its full significance. "Buried alive.

Just imagine. No light. No air. They'd be suffocating, trying to fight their way out. But six feet down? Who would ever hear 'em? There, in the grave, they screamed, they fought and clawed at the lid; breathed up all the oxygen and then… well, you can picture what happened to them, can't you, lad?"

"What did they look like?" Clearly the electrician's imagination wasn't up to conjuring the macabre scene.

"Oh… terrible, just terrible. You see, in this part of Yorkshire, there are natural salts in the soil. They preserve the bodies buried here. Only turns 'em yellow. Bright yellow like a sunflower. Apart from the colour they looked the same as the day they died. Like this." Eyes wide open, his face the distillation of pure terror, the gravedigger hooked his brown fingers into talons and contorted his body as if twisted by unendurable agony. "Those buried alive, they just froze like that. Like statues. But, dear God in heaven, the expression on their poor faces."

"Jesus… that's awful."

"Oh, I've seen worse, lad."

"What-what was the worse you've seen?' The man gulped his tea.

"Ah… that'd be two days ago. When we disinterred Rose Burswick. The moment we opened the coffin lid we saw… ah, no… no." He shook his head gravely, slurped the tea, then scratched his leathery ear. "No, it's so bad I can't bring myself to… no."

But he did go onto describe others in lurid, eye-watering detail. "Old Walter Weltson. My uncle were gravedigger when they planted him—summer of 1946. Weltson was the fattest man in Hemsworth—thirty stone or more. It took so long to build a coffin that the meat-flies got him. Ah… last week, when we opened his coffin up, it were like opening a box of long-grain rice. Couldn't see him. Just this mound of maggots all hard and white, like dried rice. Then it rained. My God, I'll never eat rice-pudding again. Look." The gravedigger pointed at something small and white on the brick floor. "There's one of the maggots. Must've trod it on me boots." The gravedigger watched with satisfaction as the young man nervously peered at the white morsel.

"Oh, Christ," he murmured loosening his shirt collar. "Awful."

"There there was…" The gravedigger had more stories about graves, involving worms, rats; even rabbits—"you see, the rabbits had tunnelled down and built nests in the coffins, and we found the baby rabbits scampering about inside empty ribcages" —and there were grisly yarns about valuable jewellery lodged in backbones, about pennies on eyes—"of course when the eyeballs dried they stuck to the pennies, so when you lifted the pennies…"—and then back to maggots, and mole nests in skulls, and… The gravedigger noticed the young man's attention had wandered; he even finished replacing the freezer back plate and swigged off his tea without really taking any notice of what he was being told.

Time to play the ace.

Sighing, the gravedigger lit the butt that had been tucked snug behind his ear. "You know, I can't get that last one we dug up out of my mind. Aye, Rose Burswick.'

The electrician's eyes focussed on the gravedigger. "You mean that really... awful one?"

"Aye. The worst." Sombre-faced, yet inwardly gleeful, the gravedigger tragically put his head in his hands. "The worst ever. And I've seen some terrible things in my time."

The young man was hooked. "What happened?"

"Well, promise me you'll tell no one."

"You can trust me, mister."

"Remember the old factory down by the river?"

"Yeah, that's the one that got sealed off with those radiation warning signs."

"That is because during World War One," the gravedigger jabbed the glowing tab into the air for emphasis, "that's where they painted luminous faces on watches, ships' instruments and such-like."

"Uh?"

"Back then, they used radium to make things glow in the dark. And radium is radioactive. They took girls, fourteen, fifteen, sixteen years old, to apply this stuff to watch faces and compasses. Course, way back when, nobody knew what radiation did to you. Most of the factory girls were dead before they were twenty—just rotted away as they worked. Rose Burswick was there for five years. She used a little brush to pain the radium on the watch faces. Trouble is it dried quick, so she'd lick the brush every couple of minutes to keep it moist. Each time she did that, she must have swallowed a few flakes of radium."

"My God. It's a wonder it didn't kill her."

The gravedigger shrugged. "It did—at least that's what the doctors said. In 1935 Rose Burswick was buried—she was thirty-six."

"Bet she was a mess, living that long after."

"Aye, but that's not the worst of it. Like I said, two days ago we opened the grave."

"Ugh... what did you find?"

The gravedigger rubbed his eyes as if trying to erase the terrible image. "Well... we lifted the coffin, it were intact. It was then I noticed something strange... where the lid met the coffin there was like this pale yellow trim round the edge. Funny, I thought. But reckoned it were just a bit of mould. Anyway, when we came to prise off the lid it—it just flew off. Bang. Like the top popping off a Jack-in-the-Box."

"Jesus Johnnie!"

"And inside… inside it were full. Ram-jam full to the brim."

The electrician rubbed the back of his hand across his mouth. As if a bad taste oozed across his tongue. "Full of what?"

The gravedigger shrugged. "Rose Burswick." He pulled on his cigarette, hard. "They say she buried six stone when they buried her. But when we opened that coffin it were like opening a carton of ice cream. There was just this big block—bright yellow. It had grown and grown until the coffin sides had stopped it growing any bigger. But even then, the pressure inside had been so great it were being forced through the crack between the lid and the coffin, making that yellow trim. Course, we just thought it were some kind of fungus, so we tipped it out. It came out like a banana jelly from a mould. On the grass was that yellow block—moist, glistening—coffin-shaped."

"What—what'd happened to Rose Burswick.'

"Oh … that's just it. It *was* Rose Burswick."

"How?"

"Mue-tay-shun.'" The gravedigger rolled the syllables around his mouth like a juicy morsel. "Mue-tay-shun. You see, the radion'd caused her to mutate in the grave. The coffin had become her—her second womb. Aye, and she like… gestated… she evolved into something that was not human."

"Did you touch it?"

"Not on your nelly. We ran like hell. But when the Cemetery Board found out, we had to go back to… IT." The gravedigger leaned back against the freezer. "And do you know what we found there?"

The young man shook his head.

"We found it had changed. Just sort of become a soft mound and, aye, it had grown. It had swelled and swollen. Oh, I tell you. That shook us to the core, it did. You see, Tuesday was that sunny day, scorching hot. The heat must have brought it on, and it were growing fast."

"Jesus. Then what?"

"We tried to lever it into a skip to take it down to the Crem. Burn it. But this soft mound of a thing had taken root. Mue-tay-shun caused what were left of the intestine to grow, and to worm its way into the earth. Just like a long yellow snake. It ended up us taking a shovel to it, then cutting through the fleshy tube. She… *it* screamed. Pain. Real pain! God, it were a living nightmare. Then—there it were—up and moving. Moving like I don't know what. What were left of her arms and legs had turned into swollen, yellow stumps, with back-to-front feet, and hands that had twisted up into hooves … oh, I tell you, lad—revolting, utterly revolting.

"It were growing dark," he continued, "and we were trying to get this thing into the hut. That's when we noticed the worst part. I held a torch to it and studied it close up. This yellow stuff, almost transparent, like yellow jelly, and I—I could see inside of it."

The young man's eyes bulged. "What ya' see!"

"Terrible. Just under the surface, about four, maybe six inches down through this thick jelly, I could see—clearly see!—Rose Burswick's face. Or what was left of it. Wide, staring eyes coming out of their sockets three inches or more, like red, raw sausages. The tongue... long, thrusting out the mouth, up through the skin until the top wiggled all pink and wet above the surface. Aye... and the mouth. Good God. The mouth opening, shutting like this." Wordlessly, he solemnly slapped his lips together like a goldfish. "I reckon she was trying to say something. Call for help. A desperate cry for mercy. You know, that expression on her face will stick in my mind forever. Sheer terror. Like a continual state of shock. As if she knew what had happened—mue-tay-shun. That and being buried alive."

"What happened to it?"

"What happened? Why, it kept growing. So we had to find a way to stop it."

"And how..." The electrician trailed off in horror, as if guessing.

"Sub-zero temperatures." The gravedigger tapped the freezer lid with a nicotine-stained finger. "Why else do you think that a cemetery store would keep a freezer?" He began to lift the lid. "Look."

"No!" The electrician's voice rose to a shriek. Slamming the part-opened lid down, he tightly shut his eyes. "No!"

Enjoying himself hugely, the gravedigger kept a straight face, but he couldn't keep the mischievous twinkle from his eye. "Suit yourself."

"I-I-I've got to go. I'm late." The electrician snatched his screwdrivers and pliers together, bundled them into his toolkit, then holding onto the limp, white hat ran from the building.

The electrician was starting the van when the gravedigger breathlessly hobbled up.

"Hey... oh, my leg is giving me gyp. Hey, you've forgotten this." The gravedigger waved a spool of copper wire in the air.

"Oh, ta." Opening the door, the young man tossed the reel into the back.

The gravedigger fixed him with a look. "You know, as long the freezer's working," he said, "nothing'll happen. Old Rose Burswick is frozen solid—like a block of ice cream."

Something occurred to the electrician. "Wait a minute. How long since the freezer packed in?"

"Ah... let's see... I saw some water on the floor yesterday morning, but Bill said not to bother, it'll only be—"

"Jesus! The freezer's been off more than twenty-four hours? You're lucky it didn't thaw." He suddenly fixed the gravedigger with a fierce stare. "Tell me you've switched it back on now? And you've got it on fast-freeze?"

"No. I haven't touched the thing. Thought you did."

"It's still switched *off*? My God! Just pray we're in time." He jumped out of the van and hurried back in the direction of the hut, the gravedigger trailing behind and grumbling about his dickey leg.

Too late.

Much too late.

They heard a noise from inside, just like dozens of loose boards being knocked over, a succession of thumps, a crash of mugs hitting the floor, then with a loud crunch the twin doors burst open. And what had once been Rose Burswick, swelled and flowed out onto the path. A mass of quivering yellow, the size of a beached whale, it moved as fast as a man can walk.

The gravedigger hollered a warning to the electrician, turned, then ran. The limp forgotten, he sprinted across the cemetery, leaping over headstones at such a hell of a speed it would have drawn murmurs of approval from any two hundred metre hurdles champion.

Luck had deserted the electrician. Stumbling backwards over a mound of soil, he slipped and fell into Mayor Hudson's grave-to-be. Down at the bottom of the pit, the electrician opened his eyes to the darkness. For something had blocked out the daylight. Looking up, he saw that covering the grave, like a lid, was the gelatinous yellow form of Rose Burswick. Briefly, the sun shone through the yellow to reveal shapes suspended in the translucent body; they resembled fruit suspended in a dessert jelly—an arm, a leg, splinters of bone, distended internal organs.

And a head.

The head turned in the jelly... rotating slowly, and smoothly, and remorselessly, until its face was turned, gradually, to the electrician.

The face. That expression.

On the far side of the cemetery, the gravedigger scrambling over a brick wall, heard the muffled scream. He wanted to go back and help the lad, he really did. But fear drove him from the cemetery as fast as his legs could carry him.

Back in the grave: the electrician's eyes were fixed on that face as Rose Burswick plopped into the hole.

And after more than sixty years of solitude in her cold and lonely grave, Rose Burswick hugged the handsome young man in the floppy, white hat. She hugged him in an embrace that seemed to last forever and ever.

And the expression on her face remained in the electrician's memory, as if burnt there by fire.

She was smiling.

WEIRD HOUSE
a specialty horror press
Order from weirdhousepress.com

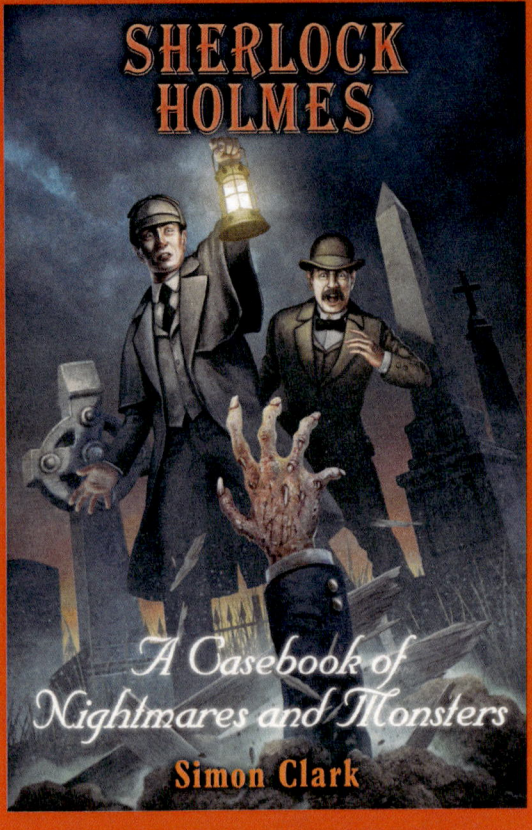

HOLMES IS BACK!

Six occult tales in the classic manner of the great Sir Arthur Conan Doyle plunge Sherlock Holmes and Dr. John Watson into a series of adventures as mysterious as they are deadly. This substantial collection features novella-length stories that venture into the eeriest territories and the strangest encounters.

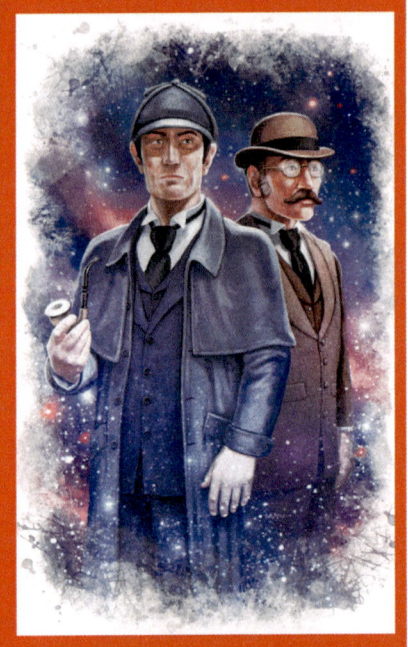

SHERLOCK HOLMES

A Casebook of Nightmares and Monsters

Simon Clark

PRAISE FOR SIMON CLARK

"... This guy is something special. It's time to find out what you've been missing." —*Hellnotes*

"... Inventive and fast-moving—good old-fashioned fun." —*The Washington Post*

"... Clark has the ability to keep the reader looking over his shoulder to make sure that sudden noise you hear is just the summer night breeze rattling the window." —*CNN.com*

Purchase the beautifully designed hardcover at weirdhousepress.com
For a 10% Discount code on your next weirdhousepress.com order use code: **THANKYOU**

Trade paperback and ebook editions at Amazon.com

Musicians on Horror

Curtis M. Lawson

Music and horror have an inexplicable tie, dating back even before middle age superstitions of evil dwelling within the notes of *the devil's interval* (or the tritone, as music theory refers to it), and tales of cursed songs and instruments date back before Lovecraft's influential tale *The Music of Erich Zann*.

The theme to John Carpenter's Halloween is as iconic as the mask worn by the film's antagonist and there is a certain jump rope song that can evoke feelings of nightmarish dread and conjure images of chared, razor-fingered revenants. Musical acts like King Diamond take things a bit further, developing entire albums around original tales of the macabre, and there are entire sub-genres of rock and hip-hop centered around the weird and horrific.

Perhaps the kinship between the two is so natural because of the way that both provide bridges to the fantastic. Both allow us to lose ourselves in exotic worlds. I have closed my eyes and felt my consciousness float away upon the ethereal notes of Peter Samuel's *Adagio for Strings,* the same way that Lovecraft swept me away to his Dreamlands. Blast beats and dark melodies of bands like Mayhem or Morbid Angel have summoned my mind to forlorn landscapes and hellish vistas, just as Robert W. Chambers brought me to lost Carcosa with its dark stars and terrible king.

To explore and celebrate the connection between music and horror, we have invited several musicians with close ties to horror to share their favorite dark and weird tales. We hope you enjoy their answers!

When I first read The Hill Of Dreams by Arthur Machen I found myself unintentionally drifting off into sleep (due to exhaustion—not the story!). This had the curious effect of being unsure if what I was reading was real or something my mind had imagined in its liminal state. The story's narrator seamlessly slips in and out of his own dream states as well which only deepened how strange and quaint the experience was. By the time I finished, I walked away not quite sure of what I'd just read but felt deeply moved by what felt like a very pleasant, dreamy, and mildly psychedelic experience. I haven't read the story since because the memory of the disorienting experience of slipping into dream states was so wonderful that I'm afraid a re-read will shatter the magic!

A few years later, I read Machen's tale The White People. While I remained awake and alert for this one, I found the story had an effect nearly identical to the one I'd felt with The Hill Of Dreams. Along with the main character, I felt lulled into the serene nature of the countryside—barely noticing the shift into the mythological realm beyond time, not knowing if what the character was experiencing was real for her or not. I didn't just know it intellectually—I felt it emotionally too. I remember being shocked and thinking, "Machen…! He got me again!"

The memories of these experiences have become a huge source of inspiration. They're beyond inspiration… I feel them always in my heart and in the back of my mind nagging me, demanding that I notice them, and dance with them. Every time I see a beautiful, idyllic, and lonely patch of land, I get called back to the feeling again…like being tempted into a faerie ring. The most recent album of my project Monastery titled The Garden Of Abandon was an attempt to begin exploring these feelings of drifting off into other worlds and times. Along with the music and art, I used a quaint poetry structure called a sestina to create little vignettes to guide the listener into this world. But this only made the pull of Machen's spell stronger for me as everything I've been working on since continues to be informed by this concept and feeling.

—**Robb Kavjian**
+1476+, Monastery

One of my favorite Horror Films is more like Real Life Horror. When I think of the story of the "fallen Angel" adapted, written, directed, and turned into 1987's "Angel Heart" by Alan Parker, I think of the Heat, the swamps, the ghosts, the gators, and the Voodoo of New Orleans.

Starring Mickey Rourke, Robert DeNiro, and the lovely Lisa Bonnet, in her first film Angel Heart, is full of dark places, lies, and cruelty, and the real Life Horror of denying who you are, while someone or something from your past threatens your whole world, if your secret is exposed.

This story shows how we deal with our faith, or the lack thereof; the things the Devil does, what he makes us do, the lust, the greed and the pride, the lengths we will go to to try and hide, the Devil inside.

It's all here, Forbidden Love, lost Love, dangerous liaisons, Heartbreak, the mistakes we make for passion's sake, and going to your grave with secrets never to be told.

The Real Horror is all this. It's in our everyday lives. No one talks about murder—the blood and the denial we wade through. How about you? If you've ever killed or lied, lived or died for Love, and you like beans and greens, crawfish, the blues and the voodoo. Angel Heart is for you.

The Real Horror is in man, and it's all around us, see what you'll choose what have you got to lose?

—**Eerie Von**
Danzig, Samhain, SpiderCider

My favorite weird tale has always been "The Slithering Shadow", by Robert E Howard. It combines two of my favorite things: cosmic horror, and white-knuckled pulp violence. Essentially, Conan wanders into an abandoned city and has a run-in with the god that lives underneath. It eschews the pallid academic yuppie character for uh…CONAN. Need I say more?

—**Evan D. Shelton**
Grave Gnosis, Bound for the Ground

When you put on a pair of pants, which leg goes in first? Left? Right? Do you jump into them all at once? You may be unsure, but you would know immediately if you were doing it wrong. If you think about the question too long you might end up just staring at your pants increasingly confused at what you're supposed to do with them in the first place.

Reading Brian Evenson is a lot like that. When I first encountered "A Collapse of Horses" something about it made me feel… odd. Not so much terror or paranoia, as much as a sense of incorrectness. In the story, a nameless narrator attempts to reestablish his home life after an incapacitating workplace incident. In typical psychological horror fashion, he makes frequent appeals for his own sanity, but instead of the standard "descent into madness" story, Evenson drags you into the character's own deteriorated reality.

Do they have three children in the house, or is it four? Are the horses he sees in the paddock dead, or just lying down? The questions, repetitively exercised in a deadpan fashion, end up splintering in your mind, leaving you unsure if any of it is real or even happening at all.

Years after reading it for the first time, the thought still flutters through my mind: three children, or is it four? Is something wrong with the house? Are the horses dead? The real terror is in the question.

—**Aria Rad**
Coffin Salesman

It's always hard to narrow down a favorite or most impactful story when I'm talking about the weird or horror genres, especially in this context where the question was to musicians and implies the cross-medium inspiration that occurs from one art form to another.

Stephen King, Lovecraft, and Clive Barker were obviously huge in my developing imagination when I was younger, which you can still tell today if you listen to my stuff. Then of course there is the wide array of independent authors and their works that I have discovered in the last 5 years or so like Lawson, Rinaldi, Bartlett, Thompson, Breen, etc… It's all brilliant and imaginative work that has really affected my output positively over the last few years, some not just from being a fan, but getting to collaborate with the artists on projects.

I think the most important one to me though would be Jonathan Raab's *Sheriff Kotto* books, *The Hillbilly Moonshine Massacre, The Lesser Swamp Gods of Little Dixie, and Freaky Tales From The Force: season one*. What started as a random communication (Jon asking to use one of my songs in a promotional video) turned into a great friendship and collaboration that ended up as a concept album used as a prequel to the third book in the series, Mississippi Bones *Radio Free Conspiracy Theory*.

Unfortunately, it also ended up in 5 years of my trash mysteriously disappearing and an unmarked black SUV being a normal sight late at night outside my small-town home. Also, lots of owls. I didn't notice them until John asked, but yeah, they are all around. As an official statement, I've been advised to say they don't seem out of the ordinary.

Jon's novels capture all the great things about 90's conspiracy genre as well as 80's schlock horror and 50's pulp, all my favorite stuff. It's like someone made a Lovecraftian X-files episode of The Ghostbusters for Sam Jackson to star in. Yes, it's that good. As an official statement,

I've been advised to repeat there are no factual events that happened that inspired these stories. Demon aliens hatching a plan with shadow governments to complete a mass sacrifice and instill martial law for global control, and the only thing in there way is a questionably lucid small-town sheriff/public radio talk show host ready to arm himself with whatever weapons and take whatever drugs necessary to win? Absolutely, I'm in for that journey every time.

Kotto is something seen less in the horror genre, and that is a true hero similar to those in comic books or action movies. Not the every-man or woman survivor of typical horror but a larger-than-life hero archetype in the vein of Creighton Duke mixed with Hunter S. Thompson. As an official statement, I've been advised to say Sheriff Kotto is a fictional character, who did not contact me to browbeat me and threaten my driving privileges due to his dissatisfaction with my performance as him on our concept album.

With all combined, the genre fiction era mixing, the out-of-the-box tropes used to tell the story, the envelope-pushing imagination, and the larger-than-life characters, these stories moved to the top of my favorites list and inspired my music more than I think any other writer has. As an official statement, I've been advised to say my collaboration with Jon was a pleasure and resulted in a wonderful bit of fantasy that is in no way true, and I don't regret the meeting in any way or fear for my life from stumbling on to information that puts me in daily peril.

*This is the official statement on collaboration with Jonathan Raab dictated by Jared Collins. Proofread but not altered by owl #4 in accordance with the rules, regulations, and standards of Malthus International.

—**Jarrod Collins**
Mississippi Bones

Gallows of Hell
– A Devil's Night Story

By Curtis M. Lawson

The city is burning. Orange flames paint the hazy, black skyline while smoke and light pollution block out the moon and stars. Every year these scumbags set the whole city on fire the night before Halloween. The newspapers and TV stations call it Devil's Night. A catchy name I guess, and I'm sure it sells papers, but every night is Devil's Night in Detroit. This shit—it's more like amateur hour.

Gunfire and screams echo across the parking lot. Time slows down as some teenage gang bangers—firebugs for hire—lay down suppressive fire at me. A '72 Matador with a full antennae rig serves as my cover. She's a sturdy, old broad. We make a fitting couple—an old ex-cop and an old ex-cop car, both too stubborn to die.

From the weight of my guns, I can tell that each only has a round or two left. Not enough to pop up and fire with. I eject the magazines. The thud of them hitting the concrete floor is lost beneath the *pop pops* and *rat-a-tat-tats* of the scumbags firing at me.

Only four bad guys left now. I already took out half. I should feel a twinge of guilt. Despite the grownup hardware they're carrying and despite the weight of their sins, they're still kids. I'd rather be taking out some Highwaymen or mafiosos, but as I said, tonight is amateur hour.

The rapid-fire sound of an Uzi goes silent. One of the assholes pissed through all his rounds. The other three are popping off with handguns. Best make my move while the heavy hitter fumbles with his magazine.

I reload and pop up from behind the Matador, a Browning Hi-Power nine mil in each hand. The gang bangers are blowing off forty-fours and thirty-eights. Their bullets whiz harmlessly past me. These dumb kids can barely handle the recoil. They're enamored with high-caliber weapons, but old soldiers like me know the value of accuracy over stopping power.

I fire one pistol, then the other. Both rounds find their target. Some dude with a patchy beard and a bunch of ugly gold chains takes a slug to the neck. The red stuff shoots out like a geyser as he collapses.

I catch his buddy right in the eye, further proving that my nines stop just as well as their hand cannons if you know where to hit. The gas can he holds spills across the ground when he falls. If this was a movie I could shoot the stream and teach them all a lesson about playing with fire. It's an appealing thought, but this is the real world, and lead slugs don't ignite gasoline.

The fool with Uzi is still stumbling to reload. Instead of ducking back down, I push my luck and train my sights on his face. With a squeeze of the trigger, my bullet races toward him like a pale horse galloping, but not before the last punk squeezes off a round at me.

My vest doesn't even put up a fight against the hollow tip forty-four. It tears through the Kevlar and burrows into my chest. The tip mushrooms out. It perforates my insides. The pain is so intense that I'm not even sure what's being chewed up by the slug as it zig-zags through my torso.

My spleen?

My Heart?

Doesn't much matter. I'm fucked six ways from Sunday whatever it is.

Vertigo overtakes me and the burning skyline spins around as I tumble to the asphalt. The world pulses with inky blackness as I stare up at the smoke-choked sky. It's dead quiet, save for the muffled footsteps of the punk who shot me creeping around the Matador. Maybe it sounds strange, but the car looks sad— like she knows she can't protect me anymore. I begin to wonder if she even starts, or were we both already dead before this fight began? Did we just not know it yet?

I'm just lucid enough to realize that my thoughts are off-kilter. The blood loss is too much and too fast. Focus becomes a white whale.

I shake away the brain fog and watch as some short, wannabe gangster in a rubber devil mask steps into my field of vision. He's carrying a can of gasoline and trembling with fear and excitement. The sound of the gas sloshing around turns my stomach.

I can't see his face beneath the mask, but judging by his height and his cracking voice, I'd peg him for fifteen at most. Doesn't matter how old he is. He owns his choices.

Maybe I lost today, but he's not going to win. I need to put a bullet in him before he puts another in me... or worse.

My right arm ignores the commands of my brain. It won't move, nevermind lift a gun. The pistol in my left hand went flying. Can't see where.

"Mighty, motherfucking, Jack Gallows!" The scumbag exclaims.

His voice is muffled like he's underwater. Maybe there's something wrong with him. More likely it's what's wrong with me.

"I caught me a big damn hero! Scourge of the underworld, that's what they call you right?"

The kid is pouring gasoline on me as he talks. He thinks he's a badass. He thinks he's cold as ice.

"And who's gonna kill your ass?"

I let him monologue and make a show of holding my wound. If he was a little older and more experienced, he'd savvy what I was up to and put a bullet in my face instead of playing around. The dumb, little sperm stain has no clue, though.

"Me, you old, white bitch!" He yells, answering his own rhetorical question. "I'm gonna light you up!"

I reach into my jacket and pull the pin of a grenade. When it goes off it will detonate the other three on my bandoleer. The kid pulls out a zippo, making a show of lighting it. He continues shit-talking, unaware that we're both gonna be hamburger in a few seconds.

In my mind, I count down from eight. When I get to four, I smile.

"See you in Hell," I say as the world vanishes in fire.

My life doesn't flash before my eyes. There is no fade to black. Rather, my field of vision is bathed in pure white.

Voices call out from the ivory void. I almost don't recognize them. It's been so long.

"Jack," my wife calls out to me, her voice echoing against the sea of light.

"Daddy! I missed you, daddy!" This time it's the voice of my daughter.

Their bodies materialize above me. They stand hand in hand, more beautiful than I remembered. Radiance emanates from them—a light more intense and pure than the white void surrounding us.

I float up through the nothingness, toward my daughter and my wife. For the first time in years, I weep. Jenny reaches out and wipes the tears from my cheeks. A sad smile crosses that face that I fell in love with a lifetime ago.

"I'm sorry," I sob, staring into my wife's eyes, then into my daughter's. "I'm sorry wasn't there."

Lisa wraps her tiny arms around my chest. A lifetime of hate and anger burns away at her embrace.

Jenny leans in and presses her lips against mine. Her kiss makes me complete again. The sucking black hole in my heart closes.

"I'm sorry too, Jack," she whispers.

My wife retreats away from me and pulls our daughter back with her. Lisa sobs and Jenny cries in silence.

I beg them to come back. I plead for their forgiveness. I explain that I avenged them— that I never stopped avenging them.

"I know," Jenny says, her voice heavy with morose.

Before I can argue further my heart explodes with agony. Phantom chains constrict around my being. Hooks, glowing red with heat, bite into my flesh.

The chains drag me down, away from my family. I fight back, pulling and squirming against the burning iron. Flesh and muscle tear at each protestation, but what do I care? I have nothing without them. I am nothing without them. I won't lose them again.

I scream their names across the white heavens. Lisa reaches out for me with her small hands, but her mother holds her back.

I fight against the chains and whatever lay on the other side controlling them. I hold my ground allowing the jagged hooks to flay my skin and the iron links to grind my bones. Somewhere in the back of my mind Mick Jagger is singing about wild horses.

My tenacity is of no help. Jenny and Lisa fade back into the ivory plain from which they materialized. I'm left alone… again.

I cry and wail and thrash against my chains. I curse God's name. I scream at him, demanding to be reunited with my family. The Lord ignores me. Should it be any surprise though that the gates of Heaven are closed to me?

Robbed of my family once more, my will diminishes. The red-hot iron chains pull me down. The white emptiness takes on an orange hue, becoming richer as I descend. The warmth of Heaven's glow gives way to heat that is first oppressive, then unbearable.

I find myself descending into a fiery landscape, but not the mundane inferno of a city in flames. From below me come taunts and jeers, quiet at first but growing louder by the moment. The voices call my name with derision and amusement.

I feel defeated, but unafraid. In truth, my descent to the pit began long before this. Since the day I found Jenny and Lisa butchered in our living room, Hell is all I've known. Fire and Brimstone will do little to make that worse.

As I descend, I take in a bird's eye view of the abyss. Varied landscapes of misery blur into one another with no clear borders. Craggy mountains. Ancient ruins. Lakes of fire.

Directly below me is a dead forest, populated by gnarled, leafless trees. Naked men and women hang from the blackened boughs as ravens peck and tear at their flesh.

There is a clearing amongst the dead trees, and that's where I'm being dragged to. Dozens of monstrous souls tug at my chains. They wail and cackle and taunt as they heave and ho.

The treetops rise above me. The smoldering ground draws near. Clawed fingertips reach up, scratching and grasping.

"Long time no see, Gallows," cries a cracking, high-pitched voice.

"You're in our house now, Jack," another mocks in a deeper timbre.

The pack of demons descends upon me before I hit the ground. I look at their faces and see that their numbers are made up of nearly every parasite I'd ever put in a body bag. They rip the hooks from my flesh, taking chunks of me with them. They tear away the burning chains and lacerate my skin.

Kicks and punches batter my ribs, back, and head. Gnashing teeth bite into my arms and legs. I'm stabbed with barbed claws and spears of splintered bone.

Something slices through my belly, spilling my guts. An impish thing grabs a handful of my intestine in its little talons. It pulls and pulls at my insides like a street magician with a never-ending handkerchief. The other monsters howl their approval. This goes on and on and on, but I don't bother fighting back. What's the point?

Finally, after who knows how long, they have their fill and drag me to my feet. Several of the twisted things hold me in place while some blubber covered pig-monster saunters toward me. It unspools a rail of razor wire and snorts I delight.

"I told you he would give me the power to set things right," the creature says in a familiar voice.

I look it in the eyes, and something clicks. Underneath the snout and the tusks—behind the monstrous visage—this pig-thing is Edgar Jefferson. In life, Edgar had been a self-styled devil worshiper who tortured kids and animals for fun. Never anything stronger than a twelve-year-old mind you, because he was also a big, fat pussy.

Edgar keeps talking shit as he binds my hands in razor wire. When I found his little murder den out by Lake Michigan he talked shit too, all the way up until I kicked the ladder out from under his feet and left him dangling from the rafters.

Before he died he swore up and down that he'd be a king in Hell and

I'd bow before him. He now reiterates that conversation with great pleasure. He tells me to kneel and offers mercy if I become his bitch. My response is a wad of bloody spit in his face.

Edgar takes hold of my spilled intestines. He rips them free from my inside and uses them to tie a slipknot around my neck. The others hoot and holler as I'm strung up from the scorched branch of a dead tree.

The mob of damned souls thinks they've finally beaten me, but even in death, they're still losers. As great as the pain they are putting me through is, it's nothing compared to being dragged away from Jenny and Lisa all over again. Let them have their fun. What does it matter anymore?

The demons beat me like a pinata for a bit before they grow bored. Eventually, they leave me to suffer in the company of the other hanging spirits. I watch them, others like me, suspended in agony. I wonder if there is some cosmic irony at play? Are the others all hangmen like myself? Are they the souls of those damned to the gallows? Or is there no reason at play in this nightmare realm?

From where I swing, high in the boughs of this dead, blackened tree, I can see my torturers scatter across the infernal landscape. They run amok, gleeful in the lawlessness of the underworld. It's not so different from Devil's Night, back in the world of the living. The types of swine that I put in the ground up above excel and thrive down here. They chase down small, broken spirits. They hunt, rape, and devour.

It's impossible to know how long I hang. There is no night or day. The darkness never fully envelops me, nor does it recede. An ever-present, wavering carnelian glow bathes the landscape.

A feminine voice beckons me from below. It greets me by name. Unlike the others who awaited my arrival, her tone holds no anger.

I cast my eyes downward and glimpse a woman of incredible beauty walking into the shadow of my hanging form. The ground ignites with each of her footfalls. Scavenging insects scramble out from her path.

Twin blackbirds are perched on either of the woman's shoulders, the same in color as her raven locks. Twisted antlers extend out from her forehead accentuating her beauty, rather than detracting from it. Wispy scraps of white silk barely conceal her alabaster flesh.

"I was hoping for a word," she says. "If it's no trouble."

I say nothing. I don't think I could if I wanted to. She takes my silence as consent and motions for her avian companions to fly in my direction. They peck at the noose fashioned from my intestines. Even with my insides unattached I can feel each strike and tear from their serrated beaks. The birds are mercifully quick and efficient and I crash to the smoldering ground.

The woman smiles and offers me her hand. I ignore the gesture and struggle to rise on my own. Her smile widens at my obstinance.

"Hardly seems fair, does it, Mr. Gallows?"

She looks away from me as she speaks, gesturing toward the endless landscape.

"That's what you're thinking, correct? That this is all so very… unjust? The sinister and sick allowed to revel in depravity for eternity?"

She waits for my response. I stay quiet and tear the remaining bits of intestine from my neck and toss them to the ground. They sizzle on the burning clay, and I feel the searing pain inside my abdomen.

"I don't care," I croak, trying to recover my voice after having my throat crushed on Hell's makeshift gallows.

She laughs. It sounds like thunder.

"You care, Mr. Gallows. You're a man of justice. But Hell is not about justice."

A tiny whirlwind of fire erupts from the ground as she twists on her heel. She walks away and beckons for me to follow. I concede, not knowing what else to do.

"I seem to remember reading something to the contrary," I comment as I follow her. My voice is quiet and hoarse.

"Forget what you learned in Sunday school," she responds. "You'll find no tidy system of karmic retribution in this life any more than you had in the last. In your world, on the very night you died, outlaws were burning down people's homes for money while firefighters are died in those same blazes. It's not so different here."

We walk in silence for some time. The scorching wind carries the moans of those still suffering in the forest of the hanged. The other denizens of the pit, from the smallest maggots to the largest demons, give us a wide berth. I doubt that it's me they fear.

The leafless trees recede, and craggy rocks take their place. Off in the distance, a massive phallus juts out of the ground. The erection stretches ten feet into the air. A naked woman with long blond hair squirms, impaled upon it. Her lower body is nearly ripped in half where it enters. Shreds of her ripped cheeks hang about her jaw, which is dislocated like a python where the tip pushes out through her mouth.

"Her name was Liz Somme. Ever hear of her?" my terrible and beautiful guide asks.

I shake my head.

"She was a porn star and escort in life. Made a bit of a name for herself."

I nod, unsure why I've been brought to watch this woman's suffering.

"Miss Somme may have broken a few hearts in her time, but she did not lead a life of malice by any means," The demoness explains. "Yet she suffers here for all time."

We turn away from the writhing soul of Liz Somme and stroll further into the rocky plains of ironic suffering. Oil tycoons cook in pits of boiling crude yards away from evangelists crucified on platinum crosses

I ask why this is so— why the misled and the non-violent meet agony and the sadistic revel in unchecked depravity.

"I don't make those choices. The big G—he whom thunder hath made greater—he decides who goes up and who goes down, and he doesn't appreciate any competition."

My guide spreads her arms in an exaggerated gesture to the suffering spirits around us as she continues.

"Thus any soul worth its salt—any spirit willing to break his rules—ends up here. Be they good, evil, or somewhere in between."

"But this is your realm. You decide the fates of the damned, don't you?"

She sighs and black smoke escapes her mouth. Her eyes momentarily close with impatience.

"Even in death, I can only whisper in mankind's ear. Mr. It's about passion and perception, Mr. Gallows. Each of us here chooses the nature of our damnation."

I think over her words, and I begin to understand. The souls that scream and broil believe they deserve it. Those that dole out torture likewise believe they've earned their place as masters. Passion and perspective, indeed.

The demoness leads me down into the mouth of a cave. The ground grades down steeply as we descend the winding tunnels. She has one more thing to show me, or so she says. I wonder if her little tour and speech were a lie. Perhaps this is where I'll meet my next round of suffering.

"I admire you, Mr. Gallows. I dare say we're kindred spirits."

She places a hand on my shoulder as she speaks. It burns to the core, but I refuse to flinch.

"Both you and I battle unjust enemies who believe that might makes right. Neither one of us would ever consider surrender nor compromise with tyrants or bullies."

She pauses near a sharp turn in the cavern. From around the corner, we hear the raucous sounds of a party—out of key music, cheerful bellows, and agonized pleading.

"You're just what Hell needs," she whispers. "A man to bring justice where God has chosen not to."

She has more to say, I can tell. I stay silent, waiting for her to finish.

"I have a gift for you, Jack Gallows, if you're the man I think you are," She leans close to me, pressing her chest against mine. Her touch ignites my flesh. It's a good pain—a pain that makes me feel alive.

"I can't reunite your family," she whispers in my ear. "But I can give you the next best thing."

My guide retreats and vanishes around the rocky turn ahead. I chase after her, toward the sounds of partying demons. As I round the corner I nearly fall to my knees.

Twisted souls of gangsters, killers, and sadists dance around a throne room. They gleefully stab, burn, and dine upon captive souls. But that's not what leaves me dumbstruck.

There, sitting atop a throne of bone is Rodrigo Aritza. Death had changed him, and Hell had blessed him with a twisted strength, but I could tell him anywhere. Beneath his infernal glamor—those spiraling, hircine horns, the dark, matted fur hanging about his crotch and hooves, and the Jack O' Lantern eyes— this was the man who butchered my family.

"Jack fucking Gallows?"

It seems he recognizes me as well. I'd be disappointed if he didn't.

Even as wrath and fury wash over me, I realize that the demoness has been playing me all along. I don't care, not in the slightest. I have one, singular purpose now— to kill Rodrigo Aritza again and again, for all eternity.

Rodrigo's crew of the damned form up around him—outlaw bikers with charred, sloughing flesh and undead gang bangers with teeth like broken glass. They bellow and squeal with hate. I reach down into a pile of bones and grab a splintered femur before charging headlong into them.

Despite their bluster, the demons fall quickly. As I cut each down, I realize the importance of the Devil's words.

Hell is about passion and perception. These souls are weak. Their passion is superficial and hedonistic. Mine is righteous and profound. They stand no chance.

As the last of the Hell-punks fall, I stare into Rodrigo's burning eye sockets. I can see his fear, even through the flames. He jabbers and threatens. He flares up the fire in his eyes and puffs out his chest like some kind of infernal peacock. Unimpressed, I lunge forward and stab the splintered femur through his heart.

I keep stabbing and tearing at Rodrigo until he is nothing but gristle and bonemeal. Days go by, or maybe weeks.

I scream in unholy rage, for my anger is not sated. I know he'll rematerialize, and we can do this all again, but I grow impatient. Luckily there are others to hunt—others to punish.

As I ascend from the cave, I see that the lesser demons—the insects and worms—now flee from me as they fled from her. They sense the change in my perception.

The demoness is gone. I suspect I'll never see her again, but her words stay with me and I know my place. I am what this nightmare realm needs. A man to bring justice where God has chosen not to.

Weird House
a specialty horror press

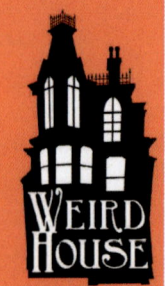

Order from weirdhousepress.com

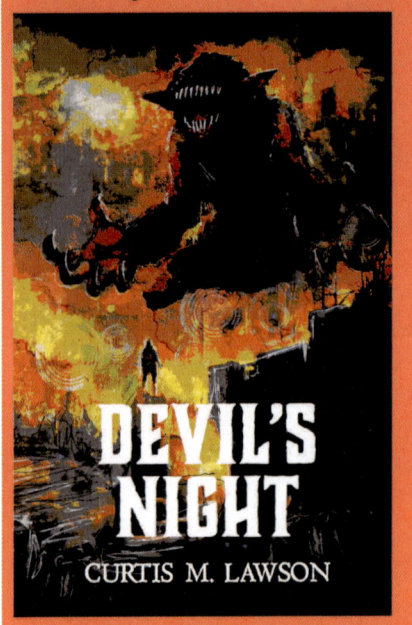

Devil's Night
by Curtis M. Lawson

In Detroit, Halloween night is uniquely beset with horrors …

Bear witness to the unquiet ghosts and dark gods of Motor City, lit by a fiery cityscape. On the night before Halloween, Detroit is burning. *Devil's Night*, a collection of interconnected urban horror tales, journeys into a dark past, taking you back to the 30th of October, 1987.

Drawing inspiration from Michigan legends such as the Nain Rouge and the Hobo Pig Lady, Lawson weaves a rich and haunting tapestry of terror and tragedy. Inside these pages, you will find cursed vinyl records, inner-city druids, diabolical priests, and slim slivers of hope. *Devil's Night* burns with Curtis M. Lawson's signature brand of supernatural dread. These stories, afire with smart psychological horror, blaze with visceral imagery and equal measures of heart and heartache.

Purchase the beautifully designed hardcover at weirdhousepress.com
For a 10% Discount code on your next weirdhousepress.com order use code: THANKYOU

Trade paperback and ebook editions at Amazon.com

POETRY

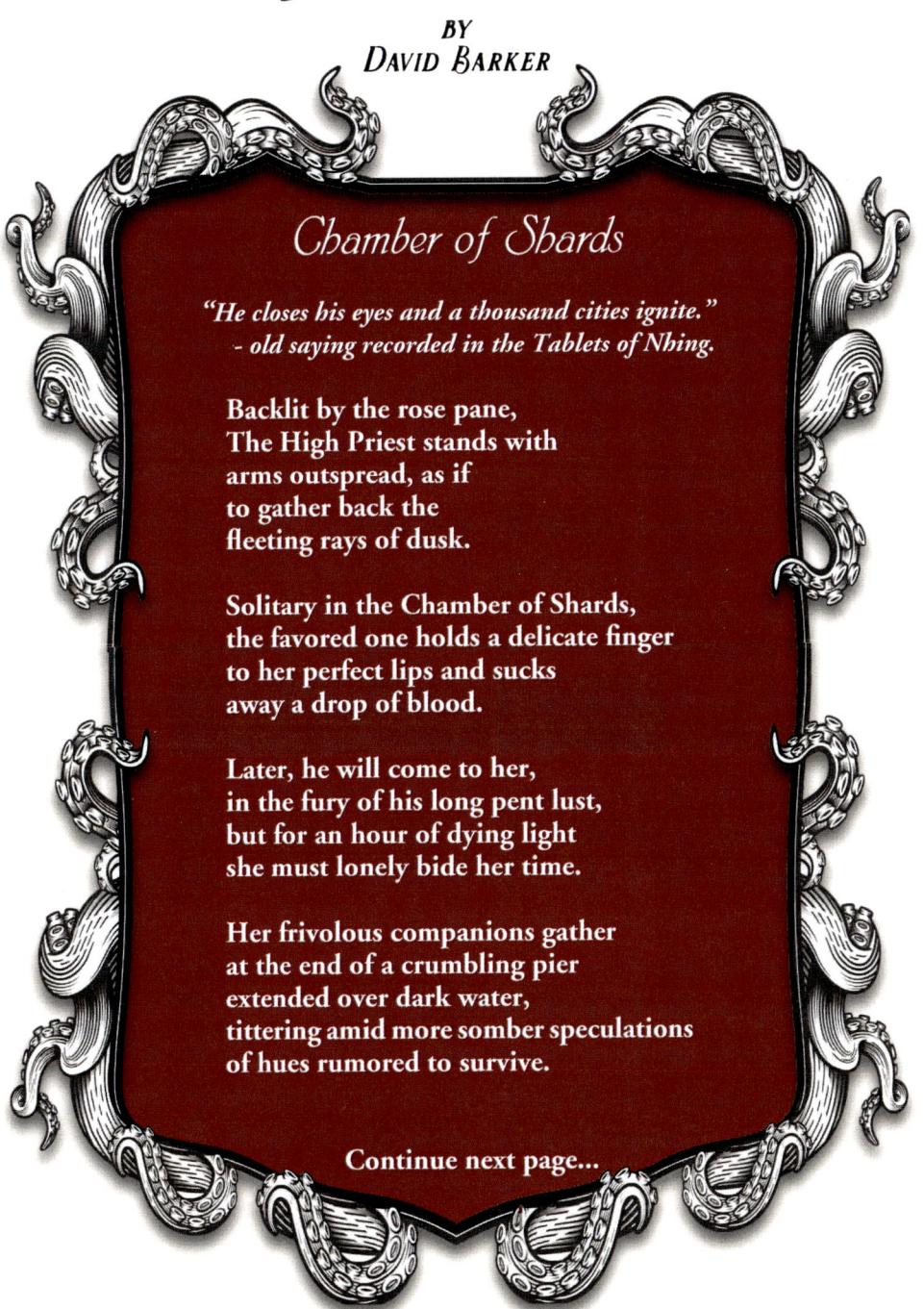

BY
DAVID BARKER

Chamber of Shards

"He closes his eyes and a thousand cities ignite."
- old saying recorded in the Tablets of Nhing.

Backlit by the rose pane,
The High Priest stands with
arms outspread, as if
to gather back the
fleeting rays of dusk.

Solitary in the Chamber of Shards,
the favored one holds a delicate finger
to her perfect lips and sucks
away a drop of blood.

Later, he will come to her,
in the fury of his long pent lust,
but for an hour of dying light
she must lonely bide her time.

Her frivolous companions gather
at the end of a crumbling pier
extended over dark water,
tittering amid more somber speculations
of hues rumored to survive.

Continue next page...

...Continue from page 65

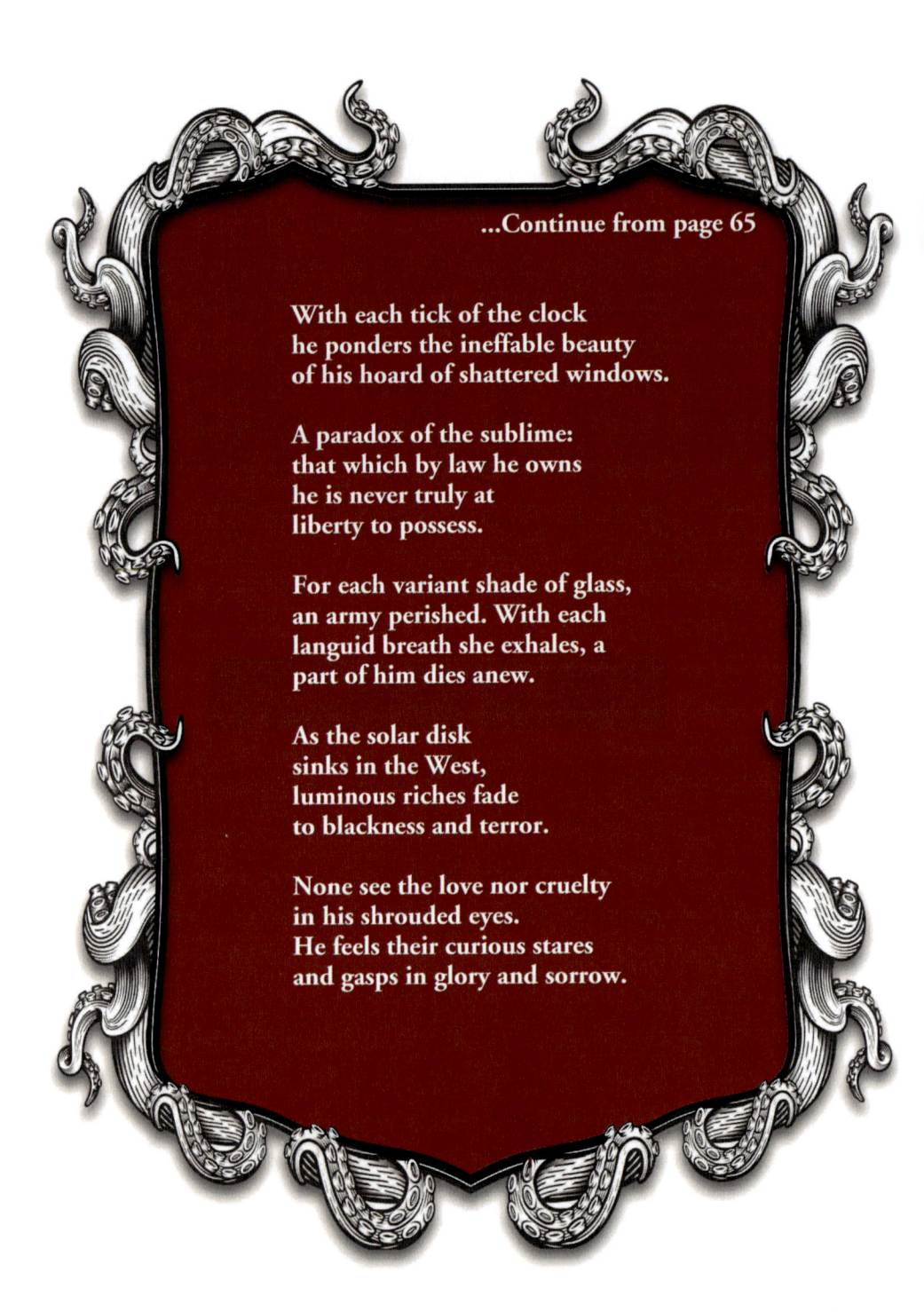

With each tick of the clock
he ponders the ineffable beauty
of his hoard of shattered windows.

A paradox of the sublime:
that which by law he owns
he is never truly at
liberty to possess.

For each variant shade of glass,
an army perished. With each
languid breath she exhales, a
part of him dies anew.

As the solar disk
sinks in the West,
luminous riches fade
to blackness and terror.

None see the love nor cruelty
in his shrouded eyes.
He feels their curious stares
and gasps in glory and sorrow.

The Crypt of Nitocris

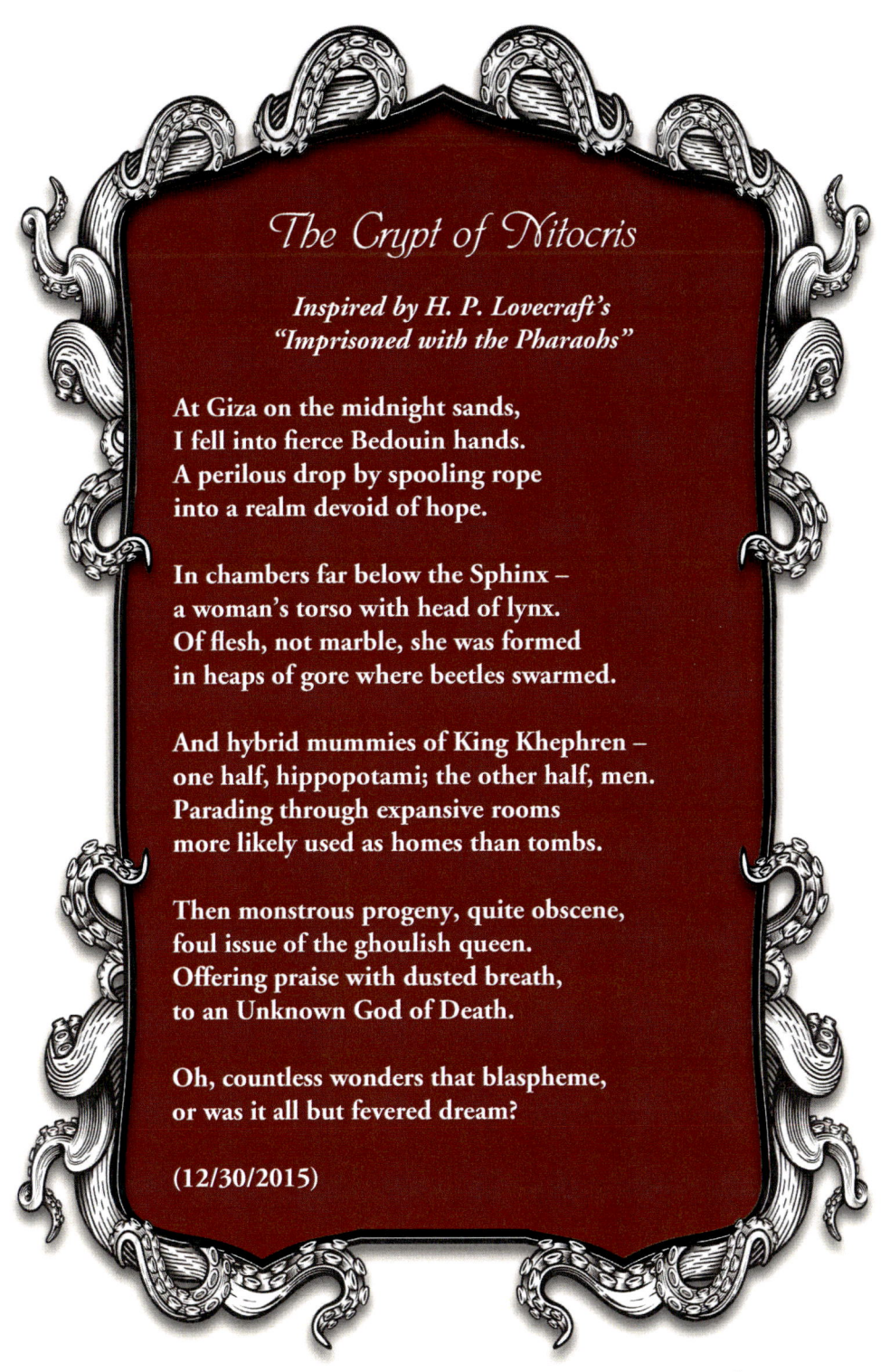

*Inspired by H. P. Lovecraft's
"Imprisoned with the Pharaohs"*

At Giza on the midnight sands,
I fell into fierce Bedouin hands.
A perilous drop by spooling rope
into a realm devoid of hope.

In chambers far below the Sphinx –
a woman's torso with head of lynx.
Of flesh, not marble, she was formed
in heaps of gore where beetles swarmed.

And hybrid mummies of King Khephren –
one half, hippopotami; the other half, men.
Parading through expansive rooms
more likely used as homes than tombs.

Then monstrous progeny, quite obscene,
foul issue of the ghoulish queen.
Offering praise with dusted breath,
to an Unknown God of Death.

Oh, countless wonders that blaspheme,
or was it all but fevered dream?

(12/30/2015)

A Frenzy of Witches

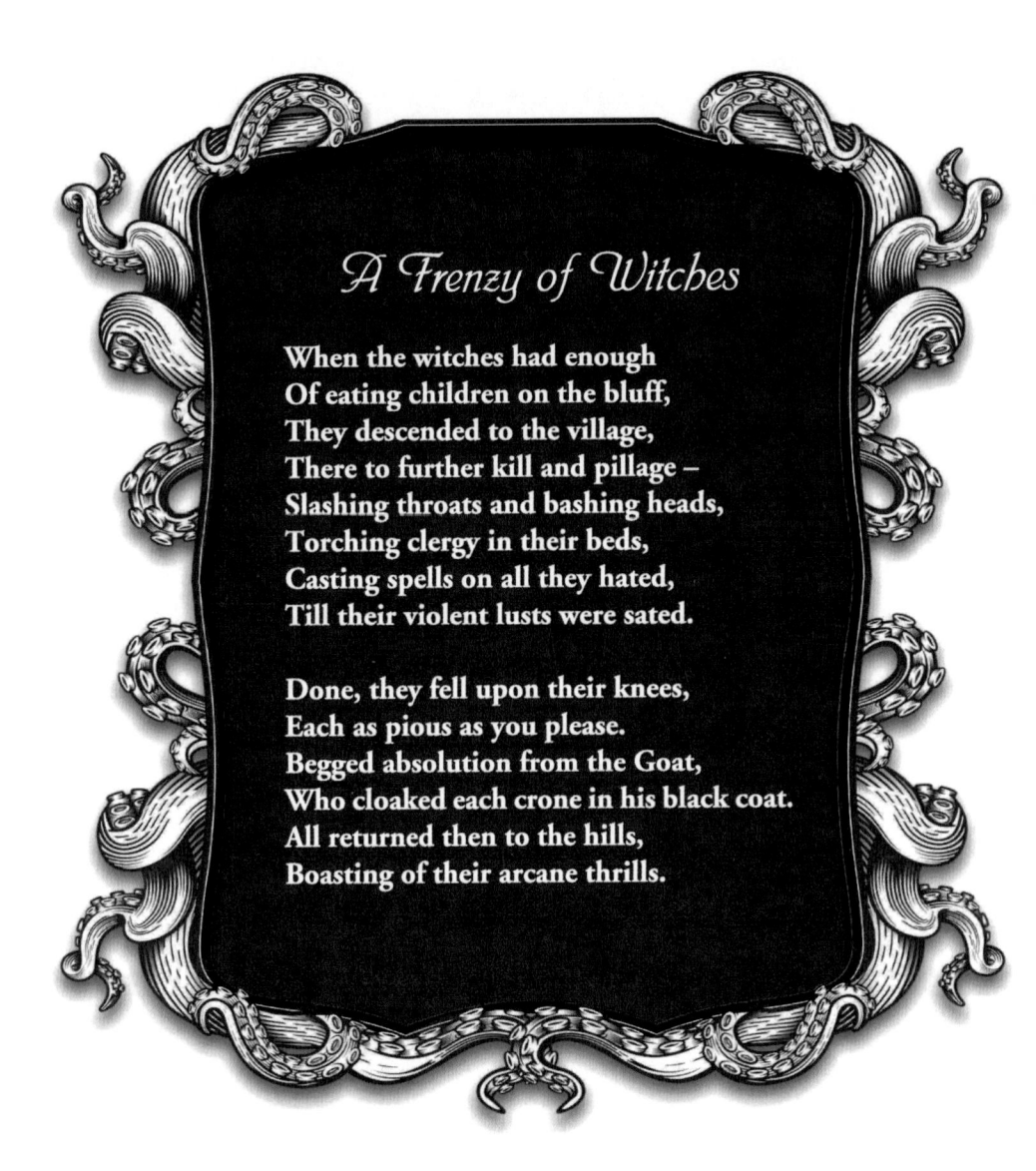

When the witches had enough
Of eating children on the bluff,
They descended to the village,
There to further kill and pillage –
Slashing throats and bashing heads,
Torching clergy in their beds,
Casting spells on all they hated,
Till their violent lusts were sated.

Done, they fell upon their knees,
Each as pious as you please.
Begged absolution from the Goat,
Who cloaked each crone in his black coat.
All returned then to the hills,
Boasting of their arcane thrills.

WEIRD HOUSE
a specialty horror press
Order from weirdhousepress.com

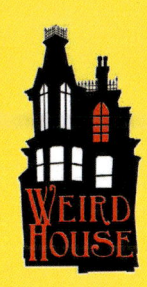

HER WAN EMBRACE
by David Barker

In the tradition of Lovecraft, Poe, Chambers, and other classic authors, Barker's chilling new collection of horror fiction brings ordinary, unremarkable people into encounters with dark spirits, mysterious entities from Outside space and time, and paranormal beings from alternate dimensions. "Her Wan Embrace" is part of a trilogy of tales set in Victorian Paris that tell of one man's battle against a horrific supernatural creature that has invaded his home in the historic Place des Vosges to enslave the minds and bodies of his wife and young children. As he is about to give up hope, the ethereal Azrael—half angel, half ghoul—steps from the shadows in an ancient church to teach him how to defend himself against *La Limace*—the monster Parisian occultists call the Great Slug. Other tales and poems reveal unutterable terrors in the South Seas, Egypt, Innsmouth, Carcosa, and elsewhere. Critics highly praised the Lovecraftian books Barker wrote in collaboration with the late W. H. Pugmire. In this stand-alone collection, Barker proves he is a force to be reckoned with in the field of weird literature.

PRAISE FOR DAVID BARKER

"… *a fiendish realm of restless spirits and uncanny horrors …*" —Adam Bolivar

"… *the voice of an abomination. David Barker becomes a creature bred of horror. The voice of the prose is quintessential Lovecraft.*" —Jordan Hofer

Purchase the beautifully designed hardcover at weirdhousepress.com
For a 10% Discount on your next weirdhousepress.com order use code: THANKYOU

Trade paperback and ebook editions at Amazon.com

Melissa and the Stone Troll

By Elana Gomel

Once there was a little girl who loved to eat. She ate bread and butter; ham and eggs; cherries and apricots. She particularly liked honey-cake, and so her parents named her Melissa, which means "honey".

Famine came to her village, and her parents died. Melissa survived but she became gaunt and pinched. She wandered into the dark forest where she met a stone troll.

"Little girl, why are you sad?" he asked.

"I am hungry!"

"Don't your parents feed you well?"

Only then did Melissa remember that her parents were dead.

"Look at me," said the troll. "I never want for sustenance; and I never grow wrinkled and sad. We are what we eat. I eat rock, and rock is eternal."

Indeed, the troll's face was as white as alabaster and his eyes as blue as sapphires. Poor Melissa thought she had never seen anyone so beautiful.

"Tell you what," said the troll. "I'll trade with you. I'll take your hunger and I'll give you my satiety. You'll never lack food again."

"But I don't want to eat rock!" said Melissa. "They'll break my teeth!"

"You can eat ashes and coals," the troll said. "They'll make you as bright and lively as fire."

Melissa who was too hungry to remember that one should not trade with trolls, agreed. The troll took her human appetite and immediately metamorphosed into a handsome young man. He walked happily away, only pausing to throw over his shoulder:

"Oh, I forgot to tell you. There is one catch. You can eat coal and ashes, you can even swallow flame, and it'll keep you alive. But human food will be poison to you."

Melissa wandered in the forest for many days until she came to king's palace. There she was hired as a kitchen wench. This suited her just fine because she could rake ashes, clean fireplaces, and collect coals. She swallowed fire and it made her eyes bright, her hair red, and her temper volatile. But she still missed human food. She confronted the chef and made him teach her everything he knew about cooking. In a short while, she forced him to resign – like everybody else, the chef was afraid of this fiery girl with her unpredictable flares of anger.

So, Melissa, who now called herself Cinderella because she ate cinders, became the cook. She cooked wonderful dishes, far more elaborate than the old chef's best creations. But she could never taste her own food; she could only remember the country fare lovingly prepared for her by her parents. And often her tears fell into the pot she was stirring, adding an additional flavor to it.

The king, pleased with the improvement of his table, wished to meet the new cook. And when Melissa appeared, he was instantly smitten with her sparkling beauty and proposed marriage to her. Melissa looked at the young king and for the first time since her parents' death felt a hunger for another person's company. For fire only consumes itself, while food is made to be shared with others.

But the king's evil councilor remonstrated and told the king those wonderful dishes were surely a slow poison. For how else to explain that the girl never tasted her own creations?

Melissa saw the doubt in the king's eyes. She took a slice of her marvelous honey cake and put it into her mouth.

And the trade with the troll was undone. She became, once again, a country girl, sweet as honey and soft as butter. But the king who wanted a spirited, impetuous wife decided not to marry her after all.

ETERNITY

by Elana Gomel

There was frost this morning, sparkles like scattered diamonds on the withered grass. Time to move. Again.

I came downstairs to make breakfast. In the yard the blowzy rose bushes shed petals. I do not like roses – the nostalgia for our childhood has curdled into sour memory – but beggars can't be choosers. We rent a new house every season as we follow the sun.

Marie started wailing and I had to attend to her. When I came back to the kitchen, Kai was methodically resetting the table, aligning forks and knives. I could not even coax my irritation into honest anger.

He brought the baby down and rocked her while I brewed tea. My friends admired him. In their praise of him I could always hear an implicit comparison. He was handsome; my skin was roughened by icy winds. He was well-bred; I spoke with a gypsy accent. He was calm and deliberate; I was impatient and moody.

I have few friends.

"Gerda," he said, "winter is coming."

Once again, the drudgery of packing; once again, the hard, thankless work of finding a sturdy wagon and a couple of ponies; once again, pots and pans, diapers, clothes, household items…

I had spent my girlhood on the road. But the roads I had traveled were guarded by ice wraiths and snow dragons, not by custom officials. And my possessions at the time had consisted of a rose and a pair of red shoes.

The worst part of our last move was when we stayed in a roadside inn. Marie, then a newborn, was fretting and I was at my wits' end. And then I heard, from the main room, the voice of a minstrel telling the story of the Snow Queen and the fearless girl who braved the white hag's wrath to rescue her childhood sweetheart from the imprisonment in the Diamond Dome. The story ended with the kiss that melted his frozen heart – and with the tinkling of coins falling into the minstrel's plate.

"I don't want to move," I said.

Not for the first time, I was astonished as my decision made itself. When I found myself on the road north, wearing red shoes and clutching a rose Kai had given me, I was surprised but I did not turn back. When I slunk out of the Gypsy Princess' hideout, I cursed my own stupidity but went on into the Black Forest.

But this had been a long time ago.

Kai's blue eyes clouded but his voice was as measured as ever.

"But you know…"

"Yes," I yelled, "I know! She'll come for you and take you back to the Diamond Dome. She'll enchant you once again by that stupid jigsaw you played with while I was battling monsters on your behalf. So let her! This time you can get out yourself!"

"Gerda," he said, "I appreciate everything you've done for me but we are a family now. Families stick together."

As if on cue, Marie started crying again. But I did not pick her up. I rushed out and stepped on an ice-crusted puddle in the front yard. It splintered with a tinkling sound.

In the Diamond Dome the light had been clear and sharp; not like the damp light of the South. It was reflected in jagged ice pieces that covered the floor. Kai's hand hovered delicately above them. He did not even lift his head when I stumbled in.

He had never told me what these pieces were.

I did not come back into the house until the sun set. Marie was asleep in her cradle; Kai – in our bed. I stood there, looking down at the face of my husband and tried to remember the boy who had given me the rose that I carried with me to the North Pole, so long ago.

I slept on the couch. And I had a dream.

The sparkling web overlays but does not obscure the innumerable stars. There are glittering shapes frozen into the floor. A banner of purple and green light is arching above my head.

My blood is not moving; my heartbeat is gone. This moment of clarity lasts forever. Time has been frozen into a lump of sparkling ice.

There are slivers of ice scattered on the floor, their chaos an affront to the order I see. But they are beginning to move, falling into a pattern…

At the far wall of the dome stands a slender white figure, its face veiled.

I was woken by Kai's arms around me. I pushed him away and rushed out into the bright night.

The grass under my bare feet crackled. The roses were silvered by moonlight. Or rather, they *were* silver. I touched a flower and cut my finger on its sharp edge.

The white-cloaked figure stood just beyond the gate. I could not see its face.

I stepped toward it. Its long-fingered hand touched the rose bush and the metallic petals clattered down, forming a word on the frozen grass. The word was "Eternity".

I ran toward the Queen, and I thought I had caught a glimpse of her face – or was it *her*? I ran, and I slipped in the petals and fell, and when I pulled myself up, they were scattered and broken, spelling nothing. The sun was rising.

I went back into the house and found my red shoes. They no longer fit, my feet having been misshapen by pregnancy, but I forced them in. The blood did not show on the red.

Marie cried again and I thought, with relief, that she would never remember me.

And I walked north.

WEIRD HOUSE

a specialty horror press

Order from weirdhousepress.com

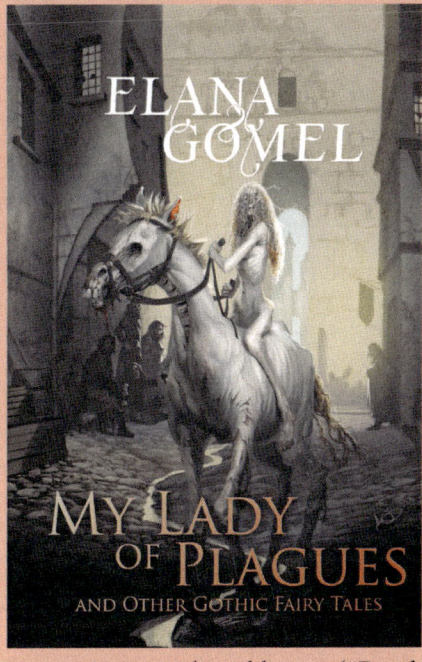

MY LADY OF PLAGUES
AND OTHER GOTHIC FAIRY TALES

BY *Elana Gomel*

A haunting collection of dark, enchanted stories …

… set in monster-infested woods and in elf-plowed lava fields; in modern-day Jerusalem and in medieval Venice; among deadly flowers and inside the body of a giant. Wildly imaginative and ranging in tone from gruesome to lyrical, these stories include new and surprising takes on traditional fairy tales ("Jack the Giant Killer" and "My Lady of Plagues"); bold feminist revisions of classic Greek myths ("Wings" and "Rattlesnake"); and contemporary political horror ("Death in Jerusalem" and "Alexei's Godmother"). Award-winning author and academic Elana Gomel brings her unique vision and her knowledge of fairy tales to create a kaleidoscopic collection of old and new stories that take you on a dark journey into magical realms you will never forget.

PRAISE FOR ELANA GOMEL

"The author creates a unique modern myth." —VICTORIA SILVERWOLF

"… rollicking, chilling, charming, and frightening." —INNSMOUTH FREE PRESS

"I really enjoyed this one." —TARA GRIMVARN

"… by turns hallucinatory, horrific and magical." —ADAM ROBERTS

"Gomel's writing is endlessly fascinating and imaginative … delightful—I cannot say enough good things about it!" —MICHAEL PICCO

Purchase the beautifully designed hardcover at weirdhousepress.com
For a 10% Discount on your next weirdhousepress.com order use code: THANKYOU

Trade paperback and ebook editions at Amazon.com

An Interview with Nick Greenwood

WEIRD HOUSE: Hi Nick, Thanks for joining us. Can you start by giving us a brief history of your art career? How did you get started? What kind of training do you have?

NICK GREENWOOD: I've loved drawing for as long as I can remember. I worked for a couple of printing companies in most of their production positions for approximately five years in all. I learned an incredible amount about the processes that goes into printing...more than any education I ever got from school. I also worked for a couple of advertising agencies as an illustrator and graphic designer. I worked part-time at one of them while attending East Carolina University and learned how to use Freehand, Pagemaker, and Photoshop. I was able to help my professor teach that to our computer graphics class, which was fairly new to the art program at ECU. After I graduated with a communication arts degree I decided I needed a change from the advertising industry and worked for a couple of different publishers as an in-house illustrator, graphic designer, and eventually creative director. There I learned the process of publishing books and began doing freelance art in the evenings. After about 15 years, I decided to try my hand at full-time freelance illustration work and have been doing that ever since.

WH: You're mainly know as a sci-fi and fantasy artist. The two genres are closely related and there can sometimes be visual overlap between them. Do you approach one different than the other? Do you find a cross-pollination between your sci-fi and fantasy work, since you have created so much art for both genres?

NG: Fantasy illustration has been my favorite thing to work on since the first time I saw a Frazetta painting...and still is. I now work on more sci-fi illustrations than anything else. In both fantasy and sci-fi, my favorite things to work on are the organic elements (people, animals, creatures, etc). However, I've gained a greater appreciation for painting machinery and equipment, especially weathered equipment. I love painting the texture and details chipped paint, rust, and dents create.

WH: I notice some compositional differences between your general illustrations and a lot of your covers. How different is the process for creating a book cover versus an interior illustration. What special considerations do you find you need to account for on a cover?

NG: The main difference in doing cover art and most other images is allowing room for text (title, subtitles, names, etc). Those things have to be allowed for in the composition and considered when placing elements hierarchically. More recently, cover art is reduced for online sales and needs to maintain its visual impact when viewed at such small sizes as well. More time is also taken when it comes to working out color choices, composition and details just to make cover images more eye-catching.

WH: You recently did the artwork for Elana Gomel's *My Lady of Plagues*, which is a very fantastical collection. I have seen the art and it is gorgeous. Can you tell us a bit about your experience on that book and how you approached the dark fairytale atmosphere?

NG: Thanks so much! It was, first and foremost, so much fun to work on. It was a welcome departure from the sci-fi work I've been focused on for the past several months. For "My Lady of Plagues", I wanted to capture a different mood for each image to fit the story they're associated with so I tried mixing up the techniques used for each one. Some were more wispy like watercolors while others were more detailed and heavy like an oil or acrylic painting. When I was in college my professors were always telling us to establish a style that you use no matter what you're working on. I always had a problem with that because I love working in so many different styles and mediums. So the MLOP project was an awesome opportunity to indulge myself and dip my toe into the proverbial style pool. I found it interesting that certain stories felt like they benefited from a high key (lighter) image even though all the stories had a sinister feeling to them.

WH: You were nominated for a Hugo award. That's quite an achievement. Can you tell us about the project that got you nominated and what that experience was like?

NG: I was nominated for best professional artist so it wasn't any individual illustration. It's always an honor just to be nominated for such a prestigious award especially when you see the caliber of the other artists in the competition. However, my personality is such that I don't like being the center of attention so awards aren't something I've sought out, but I've been very grateful for the recognition. Each time I was nominated/won any awards, I wasn't even aware it was happening so it's been a surprise.

WEIRD HOUSE MAGAZINE

WH: Who are some of the visual artists who most inspire you, or who influenced you as a beginner?

NG: My biggest influence early on was William Bouguereau, Frank Frazetta, Boris Vallejo, and Michael Whelan. I also really loved Larry Elmore, Den Beauvais, and Clyde Caldwell from the old TSR D&D days. Lately, there are so many fantastic artists in the industry it really depends on what I'm working on as to where my inspiration comes from; so many great artists such as Phillip A. Urlich, Bayard Wu, Bastien Lecouffe Deharme, Timur Dairbayev, and Ruan Jia.

WH: What about influences beyond the visual arts? Obviously you have to draw from literary sources for illustration work, but do you find aesthetic inspiration in particular aspects of nature or periods from history? Myth or psychology?

NG: Personally, music can really help my creativity, focus, and inspiration. I can be listening to some new music and just have images start popping in my head so fast I can't keep up. I really get inspiration from everywhere, though. I LOVE insects and how they work. The appear to be so alien at times. The same with deep sea creatures.

WH: Role Playing Games, in my opinion, are a fantastic place to showcase art. You've done some RPG work. Can you tell us a bit about the process? Do your designs help to inform the world-building or are you limited by a pre-determined vision?

NG: It really depends on the game system and the publisher. Some game systems are so well established and don't want any non-canonical suggestions. Some publishers have already created their game's world and characters/creatures. They send me the briefs with descriptions and just need

JUNE/2022

for me to "put it on paper" so to speak. Some publishers are more interested in a collaborative effort. Most of the time I really enjoy the freedom that gives me, but sometimes it feels a bit like a kite with too much slack in the string.

WH: Do you play tabletops RPGs? If so, what's your go to game?

NG: I haven't played any RPGs in many years, but when I did it was usually D&D. I've thought about starting back up again but honestly the main reason I don't is the time it would take. I keep telling myself that, as soon as I get all of these projects off of my desk I'll take some time to join or start a game...and then another project comes along.

WH: As an artists who works with various mediums, do you have a preferred method of creation, or does the project dictate what approach you take?

NG: Yes, the project does usually dictate the kind of medium I use. If it's a personal project (which hasn't happened in quite a while) it's usually acrylic, pencils, or oils. Unless specifically requested by the client, I work digitally for any professional projects just due to the speed/efficiency and the fact that I would need to convert it to a digital format before sending it to them anyway. I generally begin each digital illustration with pencil and paper, however. That gives me more freedom to explore concepts and ideas. The fine tuning of composition and details come after I scan in the pencils and begin working on the computer.

WH: Your resume is rather expansive. You've done work for literary titans like Orson Scott Card, game companies, and big corporate clients like AT&T and IBM. How different is it working with an individual author or a small press and a huge company? What are the pros and cons of each?

NG: I'd like to say that large corporate clients and smaller, independent publishers/authors is different, but they're all similar in many ways. It truly depends on the project. Sometimes small companies or independent authors can be more particular because it's their "baby" that we're working on. But sometimes larger companies have a very specific set of parameters that artists have to stay within in order to match their property's style guide. Both larger and smaller companies can take a long time to reply with feedback. Approvals can seem to take forever due to the smaller company having just a couple of people wearing several hats trying to juggle everything or the larger company's expansive approval process. Conversely, a smaller company can be much easier to work with because of their excitement to see the project coming to life, while working with a larger publisher you may be part of a larger team and your work isn't scrutinized quite as intensely.

WH: Your career has spanned over 20 years. What kind of changes have you seen to the business in that time? Do you find yourself having to adapt to changing tastes and advancements in technology.

NG: The switch from traditional oil and acrylic paintings to digital art is probably the biggest change I've seen. The advancement of technology has made that transition easier and more difficult. Sometimes it feels like anyone with a good computer loaded with all of the current applications can have a career in the illustration industry these days. Access to that kind of equipment definitely makes it easier, but it still takes skill and ability to stand out in the crowd. Along with changes to illustration methods, art styles have changed quite a bit over the years.

As more and more talented artists enter the industry every day and as I'm exposed to that art, my work can't help but be influenced. I think the evolutionary nature of art makes not only the art industry, but the world a better place.

WH: I imagine every artist working in genre circles has a dream project. Is there a property that you would love to work on but haven't? Something that would make your inner-child freak out with delight?

NG: I've not thought about anything like that in quite a while, but I've always wanted to work on a large LOTR project...that or do some Magic The Gathering cards. Either of those would be AWESOME!

WH: In so many ways it's easier than ever to make a career as an artist. Opportunities are abundant and easily accessible. You can find clients and collaborators across the globe. But with all that comes an immense amount of competition. What advice would you give young artists hoping to make a career in the modern era?

NG: I have four pieces of advise for anyone trying to get started in this business. 1) Do not overextend yourself. Schedule projects so that you have time to rest. It doesn't matter how much you absolutely love what you do, if you never give yourself a chance to recharge, the inevitable result will be burnout. 2) Stay happy and try to remember that you're "living the dream". There are going to be projects that aren't the most fun or what you would choose to work on if you had a choice. But, every project will have some redeeming quality about it. Try to find it. Focusing on it will not only make the project more enjoyable for you, but will ultimately make the project better because, you will enjoy yourself while you're working on it. If the artist is happy, the project will be happy. 3) Learn to budget. Freelance art paychecks don't always come on a regular basis. Feast or famine is a common way to describe it. Learn to live on a set budget so that you aren't tempted to spend everything as soon as you get it and have nothing left for the time between paydays. 4) Develop tough skin. The art world is full of very opinionated individuals who aren't shy about sharing their thoughts about your work...good and bad. Look at any criticism of your work as a challenge to overcome and use it to become better. Critiques will then have a lifting effect rather than smothering any of your self-confidence and, by default, your creativity.

WH: Thanks so much for taking the time to speak with us, Nick. What projects do you have coming up? What can we look forward to?

NG: One of the best things about freelance work is how random the projects are. I do have a couple of projects scheduled to begin very soon (a Dune RPG and a fantasy project that I'm particularly excited about). Thanks for the opportunity to share some of my thoughts. Now, back to work!

WEIRD HOUSE SHOWCASE

THE ARTWORK OF
NICK GREENWOOD

SPIRIT RACE

LIKE A THIEF IN THE LIGHT

Into Dust

Silent as Dust

Aliens

PG Man Dragon

FENRIR

Magic

Black Grief

by Aaron Besson

Alex hadn't realized he wasn't even paying attention to the pictures anymore when he realized this was the fourth time he had cycled through to the picture of his squad. It wasn't the whisky, the two fingers in his glass were still as full as when he had poured it an hour ago, it was the day.

This day was the reason that he had the whiskey and the photos out. They didn't come out of the drawer any other time. He didn't have it marked down on the calendar, that would mean it was something he needed to be reminded was coming up, or that it was something to look forward to. Neither was true.

The photo he currently held was of the last time they had all been together, right outside of Helmand. They'd been in Kandahar for a little over a month when the picture was taken. While none of their tours could be considered easy, no other moment of it could compare to what that push to Helmand had done to them. The IED, and then the ambush. He, Collins, and Dearman were the only ones who got out.

Then he took a slug of the whiskey, considering the error of that thought. They didn't get out, not completely. Collins shot himself three weeks after returning home, and Alex hadn't heard from Dearman since the funeral. There were smiles and hugs when they saw each other, but the ability to converse never got going. Getting home hadn't meant going home for either of them, the trauma had gone too deep. Seeing each other just brought back all the memories. The funeral was endured, and both of them went their separate ways before people could ask questions about how they knew Collins. There was a brief nod shared before they went their separate ways, and that was that.

Alex put the pictures down on the table and started to reach for the bottle to pour himself another. It was just there to do what it did every year; give him a different kind of numbness. He didn't like the loss of control that came with drunkenness, he lost enough with the recurring nightmares, with getting startled at random noises. He wasn't going to give more control over to something like alcohol without a fight.

At the same time, he understood this time of year made the bottle practically necessary. The sadness and the pain always started to gnaw slowly a week or two beforehand, building up to a crescendo of emotion so great as to almost be an emptiness. He needed something to replace it (He'd long given up on trying to fill it.) and Cutty Sark fit the bill. Having the mountain cabin away from all the noise helped some, he was resigned to the fact that there'd be times when he needed more.

He picked up the glass of whiskey, watched as the amber liquid moved in the glass, and raised it to his lips. Just as he was about to take a drink, the lights went out. He put the glass down and made his way to the light switch. He gave it a couple of quick flips. Nothing happened. He let out a sigh; he had forgotten to get gas for the generator. He tended to forget one thing or another during this time of year, but nothing so important as this.

Alex felt his way over to the dining table and fumbled around in the fruit bowl until he touched the keys. He put them in his pocket and made his way outside. It was a moonless night, and the air was still. He got into his jeep and turned the ignition. The rev of the engine was startling in the quiet night, but he admonished himself. His current state had ruined enough tonight, he was going to give it as little rein as he could.

The fuel meter showed he only had a quarter of a tank left, but he could refill it when he got to the gas station at the bottom of the mountain. He pulled onto the dirt road heading down.

He was maybe halfway down the road when he heard the dull thud over the thrumming of the engine. A shudder caused the jeep to swerve, but he quickly regained control. He put his foot on the brake and turned the ignition off. He could still hear and feel the echo of the rumble. Had it been an earthquake? There hadn't been one in the area in his lifetime, but that didn't mean it couldn't happen.

Air pressure felt off too. Heavier somehow. He looked up into the night sky and saw next to no stars. When he left the cabin he could still see their multitudes twinkling, now only a mere handful.

The stars that remained seemed brighter, twinkling larger and fuller as time passed. With mounting alarm he realized they weren't getting brighter, but closer; they were falling. They careened across the night sky, speeding off into different corners. A meteor shower was not unlikely but the earthquake, or whatever it was, made him uneasy about accepting that theory.

Too many weird incidents in just a few minutes couldn't just be explained away...he caught himself. This was not a good time to start entertaining notions of logical, objective deduction. He was stressed out enough to forget to buy the damn gas before causing his own blackout, he wasn't in any shape for mystery-solving mode.

He restarted the jeep and continued down the road. He turned on the radio to get some news on what was going on; nothing but static emitted from the speaker. He whirled the tuner knob back and forth, still nothing. His current mindset taken into consideration, he again suspected something was truly amiss.

He didn't have time to contemplate the situation further as vague shapes started appearing in the headlights, becoming clearer as he drove forward. A family of deer bounded past him as he stopped fast, not even startled by the jeep. He turned and watched as they ran off into the darkness behind him. He turned back around and yelled in surprise.

Cougars, raccoons, wolves, more deer, and rabbits were bounding up the road at full speed, not noticing or caring about where they stood as natural predators or prey. Alex saw a great, lumbering shape rushing just outside the headlights along the side of the road, what could only be a grizzly bear. Whatever they were running from had them all scared, and that gave Alex pause for concern.

Still looking in the direction of where the bear came from, Alex noticed something odd towards the city below a few miles away. He grabbed his binoculars from the back seat and then turned off the headlights to reduce light pollution. After waiting a few seconds for his eyesight to adjust, he looked through the binoculars and adjusted the focus.

Headlights were streaming out away from the city like great rivers of light. The highway was becoming a sparkling tide, and another dazzling stream headed past the base of the mountain. It chilled Alex to consider that whatever the animals were afraid of could be what had people leaving the city in droves.

Despite this trepidation, Alex soundly reasoned that whatever was occurring, he still wasn't going to get anywhere without gas, and his current supply was too low to be useful in the long term. Turning the headlights back on, marveling at the fauna that continued to run up the hill, he put the jeep into drive and continued down the dirt road.

He went slow at first to give the remaining animals time to get out of his way, then put the pedal down as far as he could without setting himself up for a wreck. Alex tore down the hill, occasionally shooting a quick gaze towards the city to see the nighttime exodus getting longer. The dirt road finally turned asphalt and he made a hard left

Alex breathed a little easier when he saw the lights of Earl's gas station up ahead, but it was a brief respite. Pulling into Earl's he saw that the lights were on inside the station, but the front door was wide open and Earl's vehicle, the beat-up truck that never moved in as long as Alex could remember, was gone.

He pulled forward to the closest pump and got out. He tried to flip the nozzle switch, but it was locked. He ran to the station office and practically tore the place apart looking for the pump key; nothing. Anxiety started kicking in hard. Alex had never considered that he wouldn't be able to get gas at all.

He did his breathing exercises and tried to focus; options, he needed options.

He got back into the jeep and turned the ignition. The needle showed he had about half a gallon of gas left. He wasn't going to get far. There was the truck stop down by the turnpike, maybe a couple of miles down. If it was backed up with traffic from the city, he may wind up having to push the jeep if the wait was long. It was still the only option that was reasonable.

Alex took off towards the freeway, disturbingly free of traffic. He thought it would be jammed with traffic by now, even if the toll gates had been left open due to whatever the emergency was. In the surrounding darkness of the night, the lights of the truck stop were easily visible but there was something odd about them, the way they flickered. Alex didn't have to drive too much closer to realize why and his heart sank; the truck stop was in flames.

The building itself and assorted vehicles around it were engulfed. He stopped a respectable distance from the inferno, but was still close enough to see the truck stop had been utterly destroyed, trucks and cars were on their sides and overturned like child's toys, and his stomach was in knots as he recognized bodies and parts of bodies, burnt and thrown everywhere.

A distance away from the ruins was a large chunk of machinery, something he had never seen at the truck stop before. It was a curved metal plate with what remained of a refractory panel attached to it. In the light of the flames, the "Telstar" logo could easily be made out. He then realized what he had seen earlier; those had not been shooting stars, they were satellites falling out of orbit.

Alex's anxiety started to rear up again. His breath came in ragged gasps as he clutched the steering wheel with white knuckles. His quickly eroding sense of control combined with no knowledge of what was causing all of this was paralyzing him. He tried his breathing exercises again to bring it under control, but the desperation of the moment made it near impossible. He started sobbing, trying to draw in controlled breaths that were shallow at first but slowly he started to regain his composure. He was almost back to a stable state when a noise drew his attention.

It was a rhythmic rushing noise, easily heard over the dying roar of the flames. He couldn't place it at first, but then it came to him. It sounded like crashing waves on a nearby beach. He knew that was impossible, the nearest beach was three hundred miles away. To make matters more confusing, there was the smell. His nose irritated at the sharp, acrid stench carried on the breeze.

The red low fuel light came on, bringing him back to the world of immediate needs. The destruction of the truck stop had reduced his options down to two, neither of them at all good; he could either drive towards the city and hope to get a ride with people leaving, or he could drive back towards the cabin with what little gas he had left and hope that the animals had the right idea with going to high ground.

He looked towards the city and found the decision had been made for him. There wasn't a single, shining light where the city was. Not a building, not a single headlight broke the tar-black darkness. That was it then, no use contemplating any other options at that point. He had already wasted enough precious fuel sitting there. Turning the jeep around, he started the drive back towards his cabin. That awful smell seemed to get worse and worse as he tore through the night.

He pulled his undershirt out from his flannel and covered his nose with it, which gave some relief but his eyes still watered. His headlights were the only illumination he could see in any direction and the sense of solitude it gave him, someone who practically had to be alone by nature, was crushing in its awfulness. He turned onto the dirt road heading towards his home and barreled up the hill.

About a quarter-mile from home, his luck decided to give out. The jeep sputtered to a stop and died. Still holding the undershirt over his nose, he got out of the jeep and started running up the hill. He focused on logistics, mostly out of survival instinct but also to keep from going into panic mode.

Going as quickly as he could in the darkness without risking an injury, he started planning the next steps. He had plenty of batteries, water, and food at the cabin. A lot of it would have to be eaten cold, but that was nothing he hadn't done before. Hopefully, in the morning light he'd be able to take better stock of the situation, and emergency services might even beat him to the punch. If he could just...

It wasn't just the overwhelming stench that caused him to stop in his tracks. It was the horror that assaulted his ears. The sound of crashing waves, not distant at all but just below the mountain. The slap of mighty tides against the rocks below was near deafening, but not enough to mask that other horrible noise that seemed to arise out of nowhere.

It was a muffled thumping that beat out a constant, thunderous rhythm. He put his hands over his ears to stifle the cacophony. The shirt dropped from his face and the rancid odor made him vomit as it burned his nose and mouth. As he fell to the road and deeper darkness overcame him, the last thing he heard before his moments ended was the crashing of waves on the mountainside.

"The hydrochloric acid serves a number of functions in the stomach. First, it distorts, or denatures, the structure of proteins, making them easier to digest. Second, the low pH of the hydrochloric acid acts as a deterrent against bacterial contaminants in the food. In this regard, the gastric juice of the stomach acts as a physical barrier of the immune system." -*Encyclopedia of Human Body Systems, Volume 1- Julie McDowell*

"Fenris shall rise with gaping mouth, and his upper jaw shall reach the heaven and the lower the earth. He would gape yet more if there were enough room." - *Gylfaginning, Prose Edda*

Color Out of Space: A Review

By Gary Hill

With a debut at the Toronto International Film Festival on September 7, 2019, Richard Stanley's "Color Out of Space" was released to select theaters in January of 2020 and on home video the following month. The movie was intended to be the first of a trilogy of Lovecraft films from Stanley with "The Dunwich Horror" slated to be the follow-up. Recent developments in Stanley's life (that will not be addressed here) have put the rest of the trilogy into questionable status. Based on this film, though, I hope those problems are worked out because I'd love to see what comes next in this series.

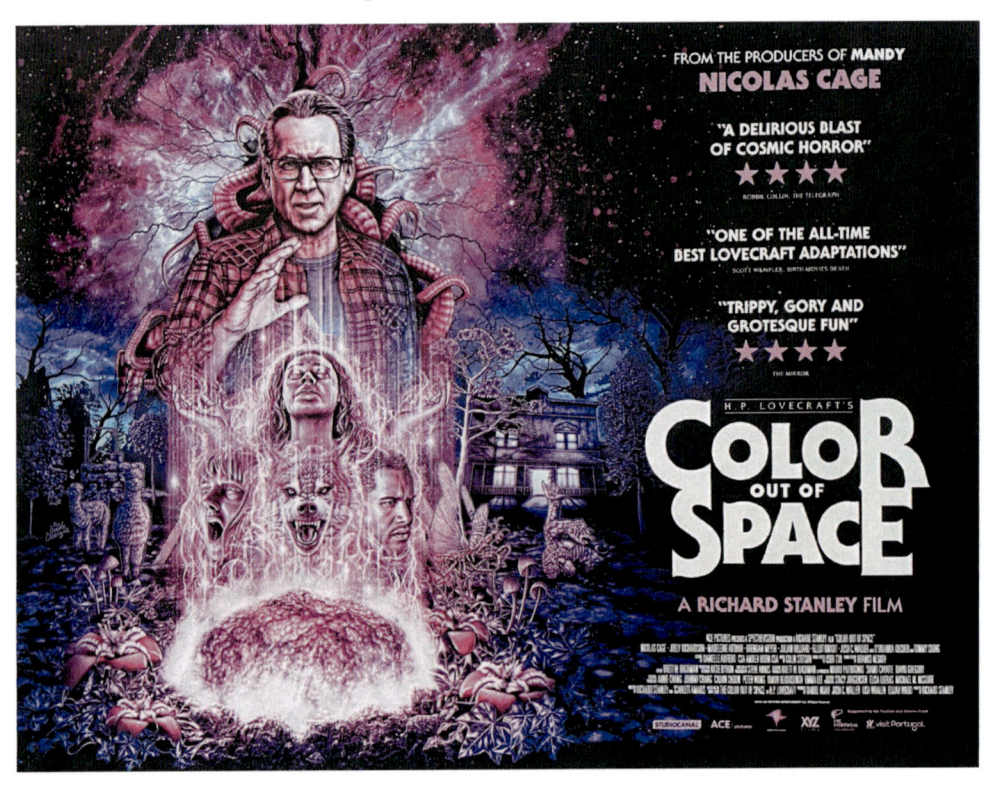

My particular journey as a fan of this film has been an interesting ride. It was my most highly-anticipated film when it was announced, and the buzz was building. Once I had it in my hands it was not precisely what I expected the first time around. I enjoyed it, but I had some issues with it. Repeated viewings has seen it grow on me, and each has been a different experience from the previous rounds. I find something new with each time in front of the screen. It has now become not only my favorite Lovecraft adaptation, but also my favorite horror movie of all-time. I'm fascinated by the film, which is probably why I keep writing reviews of it. Hopefully each new review reflects the growth of my understanding and opinion of the film.

Let's look at a few aspects of the movie to get a more detailed idea of how it plays out. First, as a Lovecraft adaptation, one thing that should be discussed is how faithful it is to the source material. How the individual viewer looks at this movie will depend on how much variance is acceptable to that person.

Over the years there have been plenty of Lovecraft adaptations. If you are looking for faithful ones, you probably need to turn to those done by the H.P. Lovecraft Historical Society. Stuart Gordon's Lovecraft films are probably the best known, and they (perhaps other than the poorly titled "Dagon") were very far from the source.

I would say that Stanley lands somewhere in between. He brings the story into the modern era, which, of course, changes it a lot from the source. I think it also makes it more relevant for modern audiences. He adds some characters to the mix, and condenses the time span covered by the story. Instead of events spreading out over more than a year in the story, in the film it all takes place over a matter of days.

Beyond those changes, though, I'd say that beats of the story and the general concept remains largely unchanged. The movie fills in some details that were not as clear in the story. Lovecraft tended to leave a lot of things to imagination. While that works well in a written tale, it's not always as effective in a film, which is by definition a visual medium. Of course, that brings up one of the most "un-filmable" parts of Lovecraft's story. Lovecraft describes a color that is unlike any other color. It would be impossible to get that completely right in a movie, but I think Stanley's answer of using a color that appears somewhere between a pink and a purple and at somehow seems like neither and looks a bit different at different times is an elegant solution. It is also appealing to the eye. Then again, purple is my favorite color, so I'm probably a little biased.

Taking it from the point of view of a summary of Lovecraft's story—a meteor crashes on a farm, after lightning strikes it disappears into the well, meteor begins reshaping all around it into something that is both horrific, but often beautiful—this film captures it completely. Many of the scenes in the story are directly paralleled in the movie. So, when it comes to those aspects, I'd consider this to be pretty faithful.

Next, let's look at the acting. That was one thing that didn't work as well for me first time around as it has in later viewings. Of course, the elephant in the room is Nicolas Cage. He's one of those actors that seems polarizing. While there are plenty of people who can't stand him, there are others who love him. I land somewhere in between—toward the like end. That said, I can see why some don't like him. If you land into that "dislike" group, you will have issues with this movie. Cage is very much what you expect of him, although I would argue that he does push the envelope a little in this movie.

Beyond Cage, though, I think that there are plenty of great performances, and some others that are more than adequate without perhaps rising to the level of greatness. I had some issues with Cage's acting the first viewing and also with the acting of Q'orianka Kilcher, who plays the mayor. That criticism faded in later viewings as I began to see the that what I found to be a problem was actually characterization and representative of what has happening to that particular character at the time.

Perhaps the biggest surprise in terms of acting was Tommy Chong's performance. On the one hand, casting him as a dope-smoking hippie who has dropped out of society isn't a big stretch. Imagining him pulling off a dramatic role as well as he did, surprised me, though. I'm so used to him being funny that seeing a variant of his trademark type of character being dead serious was a pleasant revelation. It's also interesting to note that the character he plays, Ezra, while an addition to the Lovecraft story, is based on a real person.

I suppose one of the most important things we should look at here is how the story works as a horror film. I'm a big fan of slow-burn movies. I'm a huge John Carpenter fan, and I like to describe his story-telling as "snowball rolling down a hill." This movie definitely has that sort of pacing. So, if you want a film that will grab you with some heavy stuff right at the start and then go from there, you are likely to be disappointed. Personally, I prefer to be lulled into a false sense of calm and have that shattered little-by-little until before you know it, it's in purely crazed territory. This movie fulfills that in great fashion.

Finally, I'd like to talk about the special effects in the movie, and the overall look of the film. I think that might be the best quality of the whole thing. There is an otherworldly look to much of the landscape after the meteor begins to transform everything. Much of it subtle, but definite. I wondered the first time I saw it how they got that look because it looked like it was un-enhanced for the most part. It turns out, from watching some "making of material" that the literally tweaked the actual footage to create that subtle change. I have to say that to me, that was purely brilliant because it doesn't look manipulated to me, but yet the difference is there.

Beyond that the movie makes good use of both practical and CGI effects. One stunning example of CGI is a mutated mantis that comes from the well in the middle parts of the film. It looks real, but also unreal. It is also beautiful. In terms of the practical effects some of the body transformation stuff (both human and animal) makes me think of both Stuart Gordon's "From Beyond" and John Carpenter's "The Thing."

To sum things up, perhaps the biggest indicators of how you will feel about "Color Out of Space" come down to how faithful you think adaptations should be, and what you think of Nicolas Cage. Personally, I think the movie shows the right amount of reverence to the material while updating it. It creates a movie that is at once beautiful and horrifying. That's a hard balance to make, but Stanley manages to pull it off. Since such opinions are subjective, yours will likely vary to some degree with what I've said here. Perhaps some of my views might get you to look at it in a different way, though.

The House That Wanted to Die

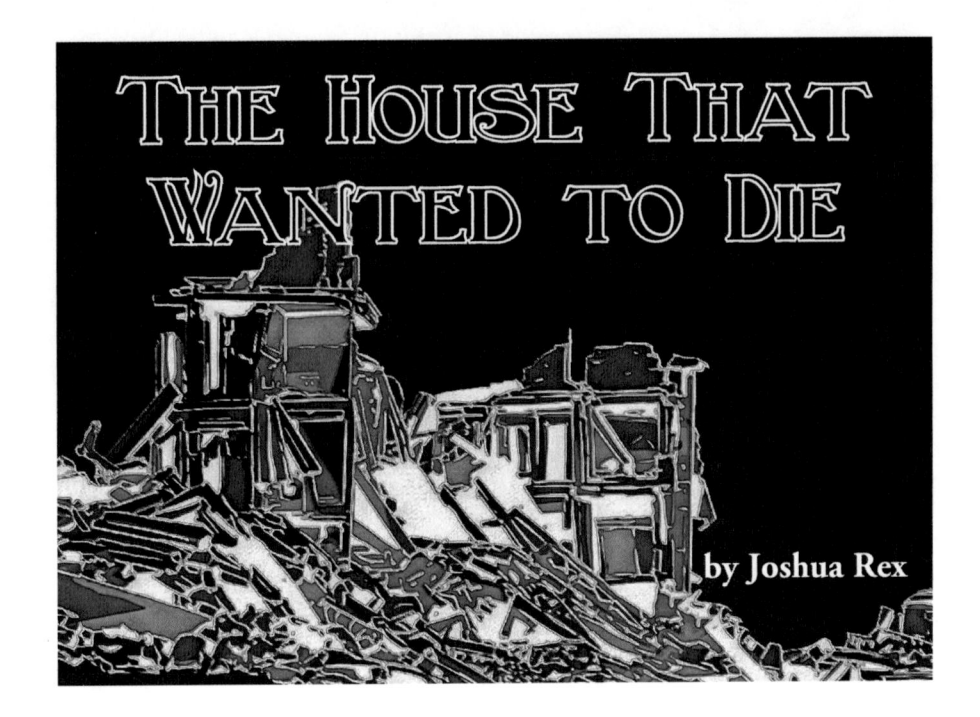

by Joshua Rex

For one hundred and thirty-five years the House had stood on the corner lot like the bow of a great flagship, the captain of a fleet of houses of similar but less grand appointments, built for the magnates of a once-flourishing industry whose massive brick edifices now lay silent as a sunken city in the valley below. This House had been the primary home of the chief executive of said industry, and from its premier vantage he had gazed out over the field of streaming smokestacks and arriving and departing trains with the satisfaction of an emperor surveying his uncontested dominion.

In its youth the House had been a badge of prestige, which the man and his large family wore with pride. Its opulence and grandiosity were nationally admired and envied—the boast of the burgeoning city—a symbol of refinement and grace reproduced in black-and-white photographs printed in newspapers and on the ivory-laid pages of expensive books. On many occasions it had been the host of social soirées, where figures of high esteem and unfathomable wealth had gathered to verbally caper matters of style, business, and politics. Then, the House's whitewashed façade had gleamed like polished marble; a regal portrait, a beacon of affluence and purity, resplendent in its prime. The nineteen-room structure was Queen Anne, with a conical tower perched at the right corner of its second floor. The hipped roof was covered in imbricate slate tiles, and iron cresting surmounted the central horizontal peak like a protective spell. There was a vast veranda of elaborate spindle work. The lawn, gated by a fence of black iron filigree, spread out before the House like Nature's flag. Inside, light strained through the windows and stained-glass transoms, illuminating the main hall where the oak paneling and elaborately carved railings and banisters glowed with the warmth of gold in a candle-lit room.

The neighborhood in which the House stood had been abandoned generations ago by those of good taste and erudition. In their place came an encroaching ghetto of vandals, looters, wantons, and worst of all—slum landlords. Nearly a century and a half later, the admiral House of that pioneering fleet was like the neglected tomb of a forgotten hero, while the armada of stately homes behind it was weather-rotted or razed or subjected to a series of "updates." The corbels and brackets, entablature, bargeboard, and fluted columns which had given them expression were removed. Common posts and metal column bracings replaced turned balusters and doweled spandrel. Leaded glass casements were swapped for storm windows. The manicured landscaping turned weedy. Plastic bags snagged like garish tinsel in the rusting chain-link perimeter boundary substituting the filigreed fencing. Within these houses, the floor plans were shifted in order to divide the internal space into new rooms, scarring the parquet floors. Drywall went up and doorways and windows were filled, leaving shadow outlines along the walls like the sealed openings of burial vaults. Plastic pipe and wire ran through holes bored into the original studs by electric tools. Innumerable layers of paint covered the wainscoting and window aprons, souping in the hand-chiseled ornamentation of carved newels and pediments, rendering their detail illegible, like the names and dates of worn headstones.

Throughout its years of dotage, the House had regarded these changes with growing anxiety. Though it was agony to watch as its long-standing neighbors were torn down, the House had decided this fate was preferable to the blank stares of the Refurbished. The newly vacant grass lots between the buildings, sunken slightly along the former foundation lines like the settled ground of recently filled graves, were in a way consoling. Though it had suffered its share of exterior defacement, the House was fortunate in having retained its original design. It helped that it had been inhabited for eight decades by the same woman—a relative of the first family to live in the House. The House, therefore, had never been subject to the whims of contemporary remodeling. Still, the old woman had neither the strength nor the money to maintain such a massive edifice, and minor issues, consistently ignored, gradually became critical. By the time of the woman's death, the neighborhood was entering a period of revitalization. The House was put up for auction, but its size and poor condition rendered it economically unfeasible to the real-estate opportunists endlessly scanning their devices for foreclosures over exorbitantly priced lunches. Despite the rise in local property values, an unsound, archaic monstrosity was, simply, a bad investment.

So for years the House stood empty except for the bats in the attic and the wasps nesting in the soffits—the icon of a departed age which, if noticed at all, was regarded as a "haunted" place. But the only things that lingered within the House were the traces of those who had once occupied its rooms, the long-dead who remained in the form of worn brass doorknobs and footstep-weathered stairs. The less obvious aspects—the echoes of voices and laughter, the cries and the screams and exaltations—were invisible, but the House *felt* them nonetheless. They were part of it, had seasoned its wooden walls like a well-played viola.

During this untenanted span, the House began to feel its own weight increasingly and acutely. Each raindrop seemed the equivalent of twenty, each wind gust like the buffeting of a tornado, every pound of snow like one more stone added atop a cairn upon its roof, threatening collapse. Water, above all, was its greatest nemesis. The House could feel it dribbling along its clapboards, finding even the slightest crevasse in its deteriorating constitution down to the joists. Its wooden skeleton swelled and dried, swelled and dried, weakening a little each time. The dirt softened beneath its sandstone base, a great composting chasm Opening—the only *true* reclamation. The House both understood and accepted this, for it had observed the new age of one-use-only transience and technological worship and wanted nothing to do with it. The House had been fortunate to serve those of a more graceful era, and it would follow them with gratitude, taking with it all of the secrets of their eloquence as well as its own like the memories of a dying man. Its one-hundred-and-thirty-five-year dominion on this plot would be forfeited, and something else would be raised in its place. Something *else*—not a retooled version of itself. The House waited with equanimity for its end. But the man came first.

Many little silver cars like his had passed the House since the reclamation of the neighborhood had begun. Always they had passed, but this one stopped directly in front of the House's yawning main gate. The man got out slowly and stood gazing up at the House. The House gazed back from its pair of shattered second-floor dormers, a ragged shade in one drawn halfway down like the lid of a lazy eye, the spongy gable above it sagging like a wrinkled brow. The man was pale and fastidious, wearing a blue button-down shirt tucked into black pants and satin black shoes. His eyes, the dull green of a faded dollar, were fixed in such a way on the House that it sent a shiver through its main support beams, stirring the bats above in their daylight sanctuary.

The man started up the fractured slate walkway, flanked by yellow knee-high grass, while talking into a shiny black rectangle. He stepped softly, cautiously onto the veranda, looked around a moment, then held the black device to his mouth and said: "Porch mostly rotten. Some floor planks salvageable, though most likely a complete tear-off." He approached the front door, which had been kicked open by three boys who had spray-painted phalluses on the wainscoting and pissed in the corners of the parlor, and stepped across the crumbling threshold. It wasn't often these days that the House was walked in—a generally pleasurable sensation unless one was stomping about. The man stopped a yard or so inside and stared, mouth agape as he surveyed the decaying grand interior. Despite its trepidation, the House felt momentarily pleased, like an old woman admired by a much younger man. His touch, however, was clinical. He struck the banister sharply with the bottom of his palm; he toed the fallen ceiling plaster in the sitting room (gently, so as not to scuff his shoes); he scraped the damask wallpaper using a blade he drew from his pocket, all the while speaking into the black rectangle: "Extreme water damage. Complete gut throughout. Rip out pocket doors for easier expansion? Potential four units/two beds downstairs; four units/one bed upstairs. Assess attic for possible loft efficiencies.

The House did not understand words; its language was physical intent, and what it felt in the man's calculating probes and prods and wraps and knocks (wiping his hands on a handkerchief as if the House was something foul) was *appraisal*. It hated the man for this, for his objective assessment, seeing not the accumulation of lives etched in the form of nicks and scratches and wear-patterns in its interior, but the potential for a re-creation, re-ordering, reconstruction, a contemporary resurrection. The House, however, was not dead, it was *alive*—given form by its creators who had built it so well it had outlived them—and life by those who had lived in and cared for it. And now it wanted only death, on its own terms. But this man had no intention of letting entropy reign. He saw too much *potential*. Realizing this, the House had a foreshadowing of the hacks and pounds and tears of an hundred hammers and nails and saws; of scaffolding rising along its outer walls; ladders tented in its refigured rooms; the slate tiles of its roof ripped away; new partitions raised, shortening its vast interior areas; its guts and facings replaced with prefabricated simplified replicas; its fine fixtures dismantled and copper plumbing removed and sold to antique dealers and scrappers; the fireplaces plugged and the transoms painted shut. It would be a wholesale suffocation, an erasing of decades of unique patina; a smothering, smoothing, re-glazing; a re-appropriation; a modification of its stout framework to suit the preferences of a culturally vapid age. The House, raised piece by piece by apprenticed artisans and skilled craftsman, would be reconfigured by work-a-day grunts. Its grace would be sealed within weather-tight materials, its Soul silenced like its neighbors: expressionless, uniform, mute.

The man opened the basement door. He tapped the black device and light beamed from it, illuminating the staircase leading below. After a few moments of silent hesitation, he started down, and as he did, the House decided to act.

It was not sure if it *could* do what it intended, but it knew that it must try, for tomorrow there would be three men, then six, then an entire crew. It could feel the man creeping around in the cellar. His footsteps itched now, like the incessant mice nibbling the House's plaster. Quietly in the rooms above, the House drew the shades over its jagged windows (witnesses of 51,465 sunrises and sunsets) and shut the front door, though a little harder than it had meant to. The man heard this and paused before crossing to the boiler. While he was examining it, the House closed the basement door, softly, with only the faintest *click* audible as the lock engaged. Then, focusing on its exterior walls, the House began to constrict. There was a deep groan, like a ship's hull in a storm, followed by a series of cracks and snaps as the brittle lathe began to splinter. There was no pain; in fact, the House actually felt relief in this yielding—a release which its square-headed nails and diagonal sheathing had so stubbornly refused. Below, the man was shouting and running for the stairs. He kicked at the heavy oak door, but unlike its modern equivalents, the door was quality, and it didn't budge.

The House would have smiled if it could. Instead, it constricted again. The downstairs floorboards snapped like matchsticks; the roof buckled and crashed down into the third and then the second-floor bedrooms. The man scurried to one of the basement's narrow horizontal windows. As he tried to break the glass the porch collapsed, burying that particular means of egress in thousands of pounds of antique spindles and wooden lace. The House next concentrated on its load-bearing beams. Using its exterior framework and its foundation for leverage, it began pulling everything above down into its center. The chimneys toppled and the old-growth balloon frame fractured as the House began to descend. The sound was immense—an entire forest falling simultaneously. In the basement the screams suddenly stopped. The House's façade was the last to fall. A swell of late-summer sunlight, briefly unclouded, settled over the flaking, black-streaked face before the latter dropped like a stage prop, crashing backward onto the pile of lumber shards and crumbled brick and the iron cresting jutting up from the wreckage like some inscrutable elegy. Later, it began to rain—a soft patter on the old rubble. Beneath the pile, the mechanical trill of the black rectangular device could be heard. After a while this stopped, and all was silent.

Across the street another House gazed enviously at the ruin through the hermetic seal of its second-level windows. Water ran from them, but this was not tears, for it could no longer cry them. It was only the rain, running in quickening drips down the vinyl-sided mask.

WEIRD HOUSE
a specialty horror press
Order from weirdhousepress.com

Music can be terrifying....

... a journal which I discovered at the bottom of a tattered viola case ... maroon, with gold embossed lettering, and two words on the cover in block capitals: THE INAMORTA ... unlined, cream-laid pages ... a fine script ... in pale brown ink which grew increasingly erratic, even frantic ... an incredible, terrifying story ... penned by a most illustrious classical musician ... the low humming of some dark and minor-key musical passage.

I cannot determine that song I hear ... is an existing piece of music. Nor is the dark melody a product of my own ... mind. What I am certain of is that both the story and its song have become and increasing distraction for me—an obsession that has led me toward an ever-increasing madness. Therefore, a word of warning to all you who peruse these pages: what follows is a sort of consuming narrative spell, and a music which animates the shadows.

PRAISE FOR JOSHUA REX

"I love to read Josh Rex. He's the poet's novelist. Dark, funny, mysterious—Josh creates pages that are a joy to get lost in. I would lavish more praise on him if I weren't so jealous of his writing."
—*NY Times* Best-Selling novelist THOMAS LENNON

"Joshua Rex is a fantastic new talent with a deep appreciation of history, an eye for the telling metaphor and above all a flair for storytelling." —ALISON LITTLEWOOD

"There is a sheer *intelligence* to his writing that is highly impressive. He wields a prose style of admirable fluency, elegance, and emotive power, and his weird conceptions are strikingly original and vital." —S. T. JOSHI

Purchase the beautifully designed hardcover at weirdhousepress.com
For a 10% Discount code on your next weirdhousepress.com order use code: THANKYOU

Trade paperback and ebook editions at Amazon.com

The Restless Quill

by Scott Thomas

England, 1887

A young gentleman purchased a house in Herefordshire's lush apple country, west of the Malvern Hills. There's nothing extraordinary about that. His motive was simple enough, namely that he wished to put some distance between himself and the cluttered, gray sameness of city life. Raised in the rural simplicity of the South Midlands, it was, in fact, something of a homecoming.

There was green upon the bough and spring in the breeze when Frederick Mullings and a modest handful of servants moved into the place. The house itself was big enough, an old Tudor with a brick-colored roof and stately chimneys. The grounds included a somewhat neglected garden and all the privacy one might desire.

There is always a period of acclimation involved when one takes to occupying an unfamiliar dwelling, and in this regard Frederick was no different from the rest. The personality of the house in question invariably has some degree of influence over how swiftly one settles, of course, and who can honestly claim that houses do not possess certain characteristics or some sort of essence that sets them apart from all others?

It did not take Frederick terribly long before he felt familiar with, and comfortable in, his new home. How pleasant it was to sit and read again, to stroll in the near orchards and the quaint village of Goodhill-on-Wye. There were white-faced cattle basking in the vernal light and tangled woods where shadows and solitude sheltered birds that had never seen cities.

One evening following tea, one of the servant girls knocked at the door of Frederick's study and stood hesitantly in the threshold when the master called her in. She looked pale (but didn't she always?) and she held a curious box of dark glassy wood.

"I found something in your bedchamber, sir."

Frederick sat forward in his chair and reached out his right hand. "Well, let's have a look."

The girl moved slowly toward him. Was she trembling? She handed Frederick the box and hastily wiped hr hands on her apron, as if she were relieved to be free of it.

The servant explained, "I was dusting in your bedchamber, sir, and the floorboards in the north corner seemed somewhat tottery, so I bent to have a look and they were in fact, quite loose. It was no effort at all to lift them out...."

"You mean to say to say that the box was hidden under the floor?"

"I do, sir."

Frederick grinned and weighed the long thin box in his hands. "Hmm. Perhaps some long-forgotten treasure, eh?"

The girl said nothing.

The hinges sang a rusty little tune when Frederick opened the thing. Inside, severed just below the elbow, were the bones of a human arm. A sad yellowing quill pen was nestled between the fingers.

Frederick stared up at the girl, echoing her pallor.

☦ ☦ ☦

The mystery was not so great as one might expect. In fact, the gruesome discovery was fairly well explained away with only a slight investigative effort. Very simply, Frederick took his chaise into the village and inquired of certain locals, whom had proven amicable during previous visits.

It seems the Tudor's past owner, Alfred Tillet, was a troubled sort. The poor fellow had hacked his own left arm off (and bled to death) for the love of a woman. While the arm was never found, the rest of the man was—a gory sight for some poor serving lass to come upon. The house had stood empty for some years before Mr. Mullings came along.

Frederick had laughed uneasily when the old shopkeeper told him the tale.

"Well," the young gent said, collecting himself. "I suppose every house has its history, eh?"

It was the proverbial stiff upper lip for Frederick.

"I s'pose they do, Mister Mullings."

☦ ☦ ☦

It was still light when Frederick arrived home. Time enough for a fine stroll by the orchards (they were a marvel of blooms just then). He went into the study to fetch his walking stick from the corner by the hob and noticed something on his desk.

It was a letter, there beside the dark wooden box.

Dear Rose,

How I've missed you! Spring is in the air and I am minded of our picnics by the River Wey. I do hope you've forgiven me. Such a lout I was. But that's all behind us now, isn't it? I hope you will consider returning to Goodhill.

Yours truly,
Alfred

The ink was still tacky, though Frederick's pens were dry. He stared at the box for a moment, then, mumbled, "Blatherskite!" and opened it. The bones were there, as before, the feather pen in hand. The tip glistened wetly.

Frederick rushed to the kitchen and raged at the help.

"I will not tolerate pranks!" he warned.

Mrs. Boyle, the housekeeper, insisted that none of the girls had been in the study that afternoon and James was busy reclaiming the garden. Only one of the girls knew how to write, at any rate, and her fingers showed no traces of ink.

Flustered, the master asked, "Well, has anyone seen a stranger about the grounds?"

"Not to my knowledge, sir," Mrs. Boyle said, "but I'll ask James, if you like."

"Never mind—I'll do it."

Frederick found the gardener in mid-battle with an overgrown briar. James had seen no one. Had he been in the house? No, he had not.

Frederick offered no explanation for his questions. He grunted and returned to the house.

☥ ☥ ☥

Frederick could have sworn he heard a soft thud as he entered the study—the sound of something closing. He went straight to the desk. Now there were two letters. It was the same left-tilted script.

Dearest Rose,

Please tell me that my anticipation has not been in vain. I am repentant, I vow. My temper is not what it was, and you are so dear to me. I would never cause you a harm. Please, my sweet, forgive me.

All my love,
Alfred

Frederick snatched the letter up. It stained his fingers.

☥ ☥ ☥

The long wooden box sat undisturbed on the desk as the clocked ticked the hours away. Frederick kept up his vigil late into the night. The moon swam above the house and a mouse moved somewhere in the wall.

When he woke, Frederick looked at the clock. He had dozed only briefly. His right hand still clung loosely to his revolver. He looked at the box—it was shut tight.

"Dear God," he whispered.

The door was locked, the windows as well, and yet there before him was another handwritten note.

Why do you ignore me this way, Rose? I have pledged my heart to you. Perhaps I may not be good enough. Perhaps you prefer that smug London banker. How could you be such a fool? Do you not see? He does not love you as I do. Don't make me come to London—it would not be pretty, I assure you.

Alfred

Frederick shuddered and pushed himself away from the desk. He stared at the box. He thought he heard scrabbling inside of it, but it was only the mouse in the wall.

Perhaps he had stood too quickly, for he felt dizzy suddenly, not quite himself. He sat back down and put the pistol on the desk.

"This is madness," the man muttered bitterly and he flipped open the box.

The contents were the same as before—the pale arm bones, the terrible thin fingers, the limp quill.

"I'll show you," he hissed.

Frederick plucked the quill out and threw it down on the desk. Next he fetched a hand bell and placed it in on top of the closed box. He settled back in his chair.

"Let's see you sneak a letter now, you bastard."

‡ ‡ ‡

The bell never did ring, but when Frederick woke, the room was bright with sunlight and a new letter was waiting.

Rose,

You have left me no choice. I would as soon see you dead as with that soulless bore. You have broken my heart, but soon we will be together at last.

Alfred

Frederick only glanced at the letter. He had things to concern himself with. He packed a bag and had his horse hitched up. He reached the train station at ten a.m.

The London-bound train arrived at last, and sat there in its own steam, as if cooking. The conductor saw the passengers up the steps.

While it was Frederick's left hand that clutched the pistol in his pocket, his ink-stained finger clinging to the trigger, the legs that marched him onto the train did not feel like his own.

Contributor Bios

Joe Morey, creator, former editor, and publisher of *Dark Regions Press* (1985 - 2013). In 2010 *Dark Regions Press* won the *HWA* Specialty Press Award. The books under his editorship won *Bram Stoker Awards*, and other awards from around the world. His emphasis has always been to produce beautiful hardcover editions embellished with art, and carefully designed to add a level of sophistication and elegance with excellent fiction. His passion is short story collections. Joe Morey has been publishing for thirty-eight years. Weird House will be his last specialty small press.

Curtis M. Lawson is an author of unapologetically weird and transgressive fiction, fantastical graphic novels, and dark poetry. His work ranges from technicolor pulp adventures to bleak cosmic horror.

Curtis is a member of the Horror Writer's Association, and the host of the *Wyrd Transmissions* podcast. He resides just outside of Providence, RI.

Cyrus Wraith Walker has been a production designer for the publishing industry for over 12 years. He holds a Master's Degree in writing from Portland State University's English and Master's in Publishing program. Since then he has provided the small press, independent author, and other cover artists with their book production needs including but not limited to cover art, cover design, typography, interior print typesetting, layout and design, and custom eBook coding, photo realistic art assets and matte painted cover art. Since then he has designed over 800 books and worked with clients such Gene Mollica Studio, Llc., in New York, Dark Regions Press, Dark Discoveries Magazine (Pre-Journalstone), Forest Avenue Press, University of Hell Press, N.W. Metalworx, multiple indie and well known authors, and currently Weird House Press.

Cyrus Lives in Portland Oregon, where he enjoys hobbies such as robotics and artificial intelligence, and gaming.

Tim Curran is the author of the novels *Skin Medicine, Hive, Dead Sea, Resurrection, The Devil Next Door, Clownflesh,* and *Biohazard*. His short stories have been collected in *Bone Marrow Stew* and *Zombie Pulp*. His novellas include *The Underdwelling, The Corpse King, Puppet Graveyard, Worm,* and *Blackout*. His short stories have appeared in such magazines as *Book of Dark Wisdom,* and *Inhuman,* as well as anthologies such as *13 Haunted Houses,*

Eulogies III, and *October Dreams II*. His fiction has been translated into German, Japanese, Spanish, and Italian. Find him on Facebook at: https://www.facebook.com/tim.curran.77

ANN K. SCHWADER lives and writes in Colorado. Her newest collection, *Unquiet Stars*, appeared in 2021 from Weird House Press. Two of her earlier collections, *Wild Hunt of the Stars* (Sam's Dot, 2010) and *Dark Energies* (P'rea Press, 2015), were Bram Stoker Award Finalists. In 2018, she received the Science Fiction & Fantasy Poetry Association's Grand Master award. She is also a two-time Rhysling Award winner. Learn more at http://www.schwader.net/

Bram Stoker Award®-nominated author **CAROL GYZANDER** writes and edits horror, sci-fi, and suspense from the northern NJ suburbs of New York City. She has a special fondness for all things tentacular. Her latest is a cryptid novella, *Forget me Not* by NeoParadoxa. Carol's short stories are in numerous anthologies, including her Stoker-nominated weird fiction story "The Yellow Crown" in *Under Twin Suns: Alternate Histories Of The Yellow Sign* (Hippocampus Press, 2021).

Carol co-edited the *Even in the Grave* ghost story anthology with James Chambers (NeoParadoxa, July 2022). HWA, HNS, MWA, SinC.

SIMON CLARK'S novels, include *Blood Crazy, Vampyrrhic, Darkness Demands, Stranger, Secrets of the Dead, Inspector Abberline & the Gods of Rome* and the award-winning *The Night of the Triffids*, which was broadcast as a five-part drama series by BBC radio.

Simon has penned many Sherlock Holmes stories over the last three decades and edited two anthologies featuring the great detective, *The Mammoth Book of Sherlock Holmes Abroad* and *Sherlock Holmes' School for Detection*, both for Robinson Books. Weird House Press have recently issued Simon's new collection, *Sherlock Holmes: A Casebook of Nightmares and Monsters*.

DAVID BARKER has been writing supernatural fiction and poetry since the mid-1980s. In collaboration with the late W. H. Pugmire, he wrote three books of Lovecraftian fiction: *The Revenant of Rebecca Pascal* (2014), *In the Gulfs of Dream & Other Lovecraftian Tales* (2015), and *Witches in Dreamland*, (2018). David's work has appeared in many magazines and anthologies including *Fungi, Cyäegha, Weird Fiction Review, The Audient Void, Nightmare's Realm, Forbidden Knowledge, Spectral Realms, The Art Mephitic,* and *A Walk in a Darker Wood*. David's collection of horror stories *Her Wan Embrace* has just been published by Weird House Press.

ELANA GOMEL is an academic and an award-winning writer. Born in Ukraine, she has lived and taught in many countries, including the US, Israel, Italy, and Hong Kong. She is the author of six non-fiction books and numerous articles on subjects such as narrative theory, posthumanism, science fiction, and serial killers. As a fiction writer, she has published more than a hundred fantasy and science fiction stories, several novellas, and four novels. She is a member of HWA and can be found at https://www.citiesoflightanddarkness.com/ and on social media

AARON BESSON is writer of Cosmic Horror and Absurdism who has contributed short stories to multiple anthologies, and one poem he still doesn't understand how it got published because he doesn't get poetry. Aaron lives in Western Washington, and in his spare time enjoys producing Dark Ambient music, comparative nihilist theory, RPGs, and reading.

JOSHUA REX is an American author of speculative fiction, and an historian who holds an M.A. from Bowling Green State University. He is the author of the novel *A Mighty Word* (Rotary Press), the novella *The Inamorta* (forthcoming, Weird House Press, 2022), and the collections *The Descent and Other Strange Stories* (Weird House Press) and *What's Coming for You* (Rotary Press). His short fiction has appeared with Nightscript, Pseudopod, Tales to Terrify, and others. He is the host of the podcast The Night Parlor, where he interviews authors, artists, historians, and musicians. He lives in Providence, Rhode Island.

SCOTT THOMAS is the author of eleven books, including *Vale Of The White Horse and Other Strange British Tales*, *Urn and Willow*, *Midnight in New England*, *Quill and Candle*, *Westermead*, *The Garden of Ghosts*, *Cobwebs and Whispers* and *Over the Darkening Fields*. His novel *Fellengrey* is a fantastical nautical adventure set in an alternate 18th century Britain. He is also the author of the novella *The Sea of Ash*.
    Thomas lives in Rhode Island with his wife and step-daughter.

F. J. BERGMANN is the poetry editor of *Mobius: The Journal of Social Change* (mobiusmagazine.com) and freelances as a copy editor and book designer. She lives in Wisconsin and fantasizes about tragedies on or near exoplanets. Her work has appeared in Asimov's SF, Polu Texni, Soft Cartel, Spectral Realms, Vastarien, and elsewhere. She was a Writers of the Future winner. She thinks imagination can compensate for anything.

ROBERT P. OTTONE is the author of the horror collection *Her Infernal Name & Other Nightmares* (an honorable mention in *The Best Horror of The Year*

Volume 13) as well as the young adult dystopian-cosmic horror trilogy *The Rise*. His short stories have appeared in various anthologies as well as online. He's also the publisher and owner of Spooky House Press. He can be found online at SpookyHousePress.com or on

Twitter/Instagram (@RobertOttone). He delights in the creepy and views bagels solely as a cream cheese delivery device.

NICK GREENWOOD lives in Jamestown, North Carolina with his wife and two of their four daughters. He attended East Carolina University and graduated with a BFA in illustration. He's worked as a fantasy, science fiction, children's, and mystery illustrator/designer in the advertising, printing, and publishing industries for more than twenty years.

GARY HILL has been publishing *Music Street Journal* (musicstreetjournal.com) since 1998. Since 2018 Hill has published MSJ simultaneously online and in book form. He also published all the archives in book form. In 2019 Hill began a series of books under the Music Street Journal banner focused on the Rockford, Illinois music scene titled, "*Music Street Journal Local: Rockford Area Music Makers.*" In August of 2006 his first book *The Strange Sound of Cthulhu: Music Inspired by the Writings of H.P. Lovecraft* was published.

Under the Tales of Wonder and Dread nameplate, Hill has published more than two dozen books. Hill launched Spooky Ventures in 2019 and has been doing video interviews, Spooky News segments and more for the Spooky Ventures YouTube Channel since then.

WEIRD HOUSE
a specialty horror press
Order from weirdhousepress.com

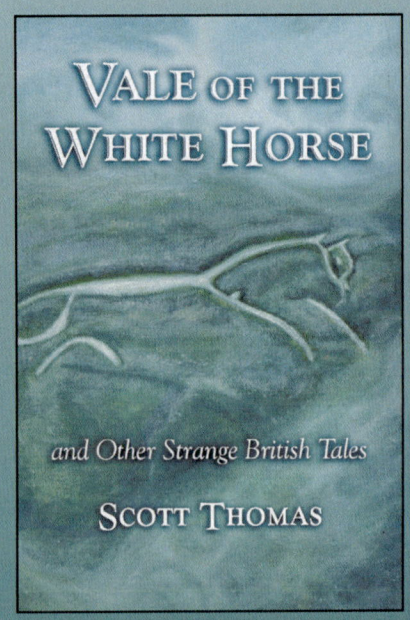

VALE OF THE WHITE HORSE
and Other Strange British Tales
BY SCOTT THOMAS

A TAPESTRY OF STRANGE AND GHOSTLY STORIES

England, steeped in mist, ghosts and mysterious beauty, is where the past never sleeps. Venture back in time to join unsuspecting inhabitants as their lives collide with the otherworldly. Encounter unsettling figures among rainy hedgerows, and ghastly occupants in a gnarled spring orchard. The inexplicable lurks in the tunnels beneath an old manor house, and something deadly prowls through gaslight and coal smoke. In the thirty stories within *The Vale of the White Horse*, Scott Thomas tours us through bleak moors, weathered stone circles, cobblestone alleys, and into the pagan shadows of an ancient land. So make yourself cozy, for the whispering dead bring a chill.

PRAISE FOR SCOTT THOMAS

"Scott Thomas has never failed me. I have long admired his dark imagination.... His horrors are all first-rate."
—WILUM HOPFROG PUGMIRE

"Thomas' sensitivity, tempered by darkness, is his strength...." —JEFF VANDERMEER

"In his stories, one always feels like it's Halloween, that time when the lines blur between our world ... and another one." —MIKE DAVIS

"... a master fantasist and one of the best weird writers of our time.... elegant darkness, intense imagination, and beautiful prose." —CURTIS M. LAWSON

Purchase the beautifully designed hardcover at weirdhousepress.com
For a 10% Discount code on your next weirdhousepress.com order use code: THANKYOU

Trade paperback and ebook editions at Amazon.com